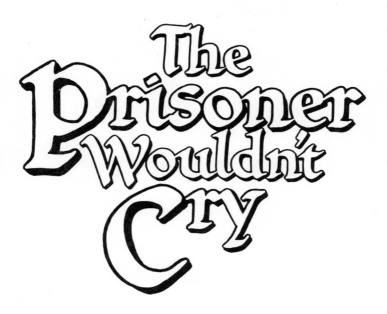

The Prisoner Wouldn't Cry

Edward E. White

Pacific Press Publishing Association
Boise, Idaho
Montemorelos, Nuevo Leon, Mexico
Oshawa, Ontario, Canada

Designed by Tim Larson
Cover photo by Duane Tank

Copyright © 1984 by
Pacific Press Publishing Association
Printed in United States of America

Library of Congress Cataloging in Publication Data

White, Edward E.
  The prisoner wouldn't cry.

  1. Bible. N.T. Timothy, 2nd—Criticism, interpretation, etc. I. Title.
BS2745.2.W45   1984   227'.8406   84-16671

ISBN 0-8163-0588-9

85 86 87 88 89 • 6 5 4 3 2 1

Contents

1. The Family of God   9

2. A Young Missionary   17

3. God's Gifts   25

4. Unashamed   35

5. Called According to Grace   45

6. Soldier, Athlete, Farmer   55

7. The Word of God   65

8. Human Philosophy   75

9. Vessels of Honor   83

10. Christian Virtues   91

11. Avoiding Apostasy   101

12. Keeping the Faith   111

13. The Christian's Hope   119

Introduction

Prison is a lonely and discouraging place. Paul is locked up in one on transparently fabricated charges.

If his second letter to Timothy had complained about unfair treatment and the disappointing end of God's faithful workers, he could easily have been pardoned. Not only is he in jail, he has been condemned to death—after serving the Lord faithfully for many years.

But there isn't a complaint or a sigh in the whole epistle! This prisoner refuses to cry! His entire letter breathes confidence and courage and victory!

Paul actually urges his young friend to be a "partaker of the afflictions of the gospel"! Certainly Timothy must not draw back on account of his suffering. "Continue thou in the things which thou hast learned," says Paul. "Preach the word. . . . Do the work of an evangelist." There must be no fear or weakness, for "God has not given us the spirit of fear; but of power."

Paul has found God faithful in many a previous trial, and he trusts Him in this one. "I know whom I have believed, and am persuaded that he is able to keep that which I have committed unto him."

His lifework will not be cut short by his imprisonment, for "the word of God is not bound." The work he dedicated his life to accomplish will go forward after his death—ever growing and enlarging!

Must he die? Yes, but, in a larger sense, "Christ . . . hath abolished death, and hath brought life and immortality to light through the gospel." "It is a faithful saying," he reminds the younger worker, that "if we be dead with him, we shall also live with him: if we suffer, we shall also reign with him."

The Roman emperor has unjustly convicted him of behavior worthy of the worst of punishments, but Paul's answer still rings down the years: "I have fought a good fight, I have finished my course, I have kept the faith: henceforth there is laid up for me a crown of righteousness, which the Lord, the righteous judge, shall give me at that day: and not to me only, but unto all them also that love his appearing."

Well may we say, What manner of man suffers so courageously? Second Timothy is Paul's final written statement and contains much of his life's philosophy, the basis of his faith—good enough reasons for our close attention. As you read this book you hold in your hand, may the faith that supported Paul so well grow in your heart till it supports you too, whenever you need it.

The Family of God

A prison is a lonely place; a death cell, lonelier still. But there is no loneliness in the letter Paul wrote his young friend Timothy from the Roman dungeon where he awaited execution.

He begins by addressing Timothy as "my dearly beloved son." A little later he again refers to him in a fatherly way as "my son." Chapter 1:2; 2:1.

The concept that church members and fellow workers are not mere friends or business partners but loving members of the family of Christ is a theme Paul had frequently developed in earlier epistles, and it returns now to fill his empty cell with love and companionship.

The family of heaven.

Paul's family included all the heavenly hosts. When writing to the Ephesians, Paul referred to "the Father of our Lord Jesus Christ, of whom the whole family in heaven and earth is named." Ephesians 3:14, 15. Obviously, Christ's family includes created beings whose habitation is in heaven and on other worlds.

No doubt Paul was acquainted with the reference to these beings in Job 38:7, where the "morning stars"—otherwise known as the "sons of God"—exult in song at the creation of our earth. Verse 4.

Like so many families on earth, the heavenly family is not without tension. The author of Job also describes an occasion when the sons of God came before the Lord. Satan came with them (Job 1:6) in order to accuse a God-fearing man of self-serving. In doing this, Satan repeated the same sort of unjust accusations against the government of God which had led earlier to his expulsion from the heavenly courts together with the angels who had taken his side.

Reading between the lines, we see the unfallen beings assembled before Jehovah as representatives of the unfallen worlds. Satan has been permitted to join them in his capacity as "prince of this world," for Adam had delivered his stewardship to him.

Even the loyal angels did not fully understand God's method of dealing with the apostasy in heaven. Not until the cross, when Satan's malevolent character was fully revealed, did they realize His way of forbearance and love. Several years before his final imprisonment, Paul himself had explained to the Colossians that "it pleased the Father . . . by him [Christ] to reconcile all things unto himself, . . . whether they be things in earth, or things in heaven." Colossians 1:19, 20. This reconciliation anticipates a grand family reunion of creatures on earth with creatures of different orders of beings in heaven and on other worlds.

Sadly, part of that family is forever lost; for while in the ages before sin entered, "all created beings acknowledged the allegiance of love, [and] there was perfect harmony throughout the universe of God, a change came over this happy state."—*Patriarchs and Prophets*, p. 35. "God's government included not only the inhabitants of heaven, but of all the worlds that He had created; and Lucifer had concluded that if he could carry the angels of heaven with him in rebellion, he could carry also all the worlds."—*Ibid*., p. 41. Satan deceived a multitude of angels, until he was put out of heaven. Then, "no longer free to stir up rebellion in heaven, Satan's enmity against God found a new field in plotting the ruin of the human race."—*Ibid*., p. 52.

The family reunited.

As a safeguard against the perpetual existence of sin, God put into operation His plan to save the deceived inhabitants of earth who had not had the opportunity to dwell in the open presence of the Godhead. This rescue plan was bitterly opposed by Satan, but thanks to the gift of the Lord Jesus Christ and His grace, it will succeed. All among the lost family of Adam who are willing will be restored to God's family. They will take the place of Satan and his expelled angels. Satan will realize—too late—that God's plan was just.

The wonderful love of God for His repentant mortals is an object lesson to the universe and will ensure "that the justice and mercy of God and the immutability of his law might be forever placed beyond all question."—*Patriarchs and Prophets*, p. 42. "By the power of His love, through obedience, fallen man, a worm of the dust, is to be transformed, fitted to be a member of the heavenly family, a companion through eternal ages of God and Christ and the holy angels. Heaven will triumph, for the vacancies made by the fall of Satan and his host will be filled by the redeemed of the Lord."—Ellen G. White, *The Upward Look*, p. 61.

What a glorious family reunion awaits the faithful when Christ takes up His kingdom to reign for ever! It is clear that one secret of Paul's courage was that he expected to be present at that reunion. Separated by sin and doomed to mortality, he knew better than we do that humanity is earthbound. The astounding scientific progress that we have seen place men on the moon and let others float freely in space is but kindergarten fumbling compared to God's plans for the restoration of His united family. Then "all the treasures of the universe will be open to the study of God's redeemed. Unfettered by mortality, they wing their tireless flight to worlds afar—worlds that thrilled with sorrow at the spectacle of human woe and rang with songs of gladness at the tidings of a ransomed soul. With unutterable delight the children of earth enter into the joy and the wisdom of unfallen beings."—*The Great Controversy*, p. 677. What a family to belong to, embracing all of God's creation, inhabiting a sinless universe, with love and harmony the ruling principle, and service to God the supreme passion of every living being!

The family of earth.

God's great family was to be increased. This creative work would demonstrate Christ's supremacy and refute Lucifer's assertion that he was Christ's equal. Because Christ had created "all the hosts of heaven, . . . to Him, as well as to God, their homage and allegiance were due. Christ was still to exercise divine power, in the creation of the earth and its inhabitants."—*Patriarchs and Prophets*, p. 36.

Before sin entered the Garden of Eden, Adam and Eve were part of God's family; but alas, after they were expelled and gave birth to sons and daughters, their ever-growing family was estranged from God. Due entirely to the sacrifice of Christ on man's behalf, humanity was given a second chance, an opportunity to reenter paradise. Christ was the link between God's family and the earthly, mortal family.

When Jacob was homeless, exiled from his father and mother, hated by his twin brother, he was also estranged from God by his deceit. But there was still contact through Jesus Christ, as Jesus Himself later explained to Nathanael. See John 1:51. The Son of God was the ladder by which angels that excel in strength ministered to this heir of salvation. See Hebrews 1:14.

> As to the homeless patriarch
> That wondrous dream was given,
> So seems my Saviour's cross to me,
> A ladder up to heaven.
> —Elizabeth C. Clephane, *The New Advent Hymnal*, no. 408.

How can rebels against God's government, men and women who are tempted by Satan and who often succumb to his devices, be called heirs? Having renounced their father, the devil, they are now orphans, fatherless.

Those who are blessed with parents for a large part of their lives find it difficult to appreciate the feelings of those others who are orphaned early. Their plight is described in a hymn written by the architect and philanthropist, James Edmeston, a benefactor of the London Orphan Asylum. In 1821 he wrote a special prayer for the annual speech day at that institution, when boys and girls were leaving the care of the orphanage to go out into the cold, hard world. The author commits them to the care of their new parents, the Father, the Saviour, and the Holy Spirit, giving one stanza for each member of the Trinity. How appropriate are his words, especially for orphans:

> Guard us, guide us, keep us, feed us,
> For we have no help but Thee.

These orphans are also described as

Yet possessing
Every blessing,
If our God our Father be.
—*The Church Hymnal, no. 87.*

Jesus came to restore repentant sinners to His family. He takes fatherless orphans who want to flee the kingdom of lies and deceit and long for the kingdom of love and trust, and He adopts them into His family. His Father becomes their Father.

Our Lord made it quite evident during His earthly ministry that as a divine-human Being, He enjoyed with God a Father-Son relationship. In the Gospels, He refers to God as "My Father" more than 150 times. He invites the orphans of earth to call His Father "our Father." And when speaking to men and women He referred to God as "your Father" at least 25 times.

Some childless couples have adopted sons or daughters and then been perplexed how to explain to the adopted children that they are not their natural parents. The most successful explanation has been that natural parents have to take what comes; whereas a child who has been adopted has been *chosen*, picked out from others, willingly and lovingly brought into the family and given the name, the privileges, the inheritance, and all else that goes with sonship and daughtership. This is what God has done for us as Christians.

A comment of Jesus to His seventy disciples is most significant. When they returned from their first missionary venture, the seventy were thrilled with their success. They had healed the sick and even cast out devils! Jesus told them that there was something far more important than miracle-working, great as that was. He said, "Rather rejoice, because your names are written in heaven." Luke 10:20.

Just as a newborn infant has his name inscribed on his birth certificate, so those who experience the new birth by water and the Spirit have their names inscribed "in the book of life of the Lamb slain from the foundation of the world." Revelation 13:8. The family of earth is therefore inextricably united through the Lamb, the

Son of God, with the original family of heaven, never to be separated. The tempter, the father of lies, the murderer, will be annihilated, and God's family will enjoy happiness for ever more.

Family ties.

The noun *tie* indicates something that joins two things together, whether in the physical world, as in rafters connected to beams in a building, or in the abstract sense, as in obligations to persons or to agreements. The ties that bind us to our families are those of blood relationship, and those that connect us to the heavenly family are those of the shed blood of divine love. The Scottish minister and hymn writer, James Grindlay, expressed it well:

> He drew me with the cords of love,
> And thus He bound me to Him.
> And 'round my heart still closely twine
> Those ties which naught can sever.
> —*The Church Hymnal*, no. 531.

This bond of love on the part of the Saviour and of obedience on the part of the believer is the cement of an unbreakable union. The twofold aspect was plainly seen one day when Jesus was speaking to the multitudes. Standing on the edge of the crowd, His mother and His half-brothers wished to speak to Him. On being informed that they were there, Jesus asked the rhetorical question, "Who is my mother? and who are my brethren?" Matthew 12:48. His answer applies to the end of time: "Whosoever shall do the will of my Father which is in heaven, the same is my brother, and sister, and mother." Verse 50.

A practical example of what Jesus meant was His relationship to Lazarus of Bethany and his sisters, Mary and Martha. While "foxes have holes, and the birds of the air have nests" (Matthew 8:20), Jesus had no home to call His own after He began His ministry. But He found shelter and a responsive spirit in Bethany. "There was one home that He loved to visit,—the home of Lazarus, and Mary, and Martha; for in the atmosphere of faith and love His spirit had rest."—*The Desire of Ages*, p. 326.

Here was an excellent example of the family tie, deeper even than that between members of the same human family. This tender relationship brings us into a much wider circle of brothers and sisters, mothers and fathers, for "if we . . . hold the relation of kinship to Him, with what tenderness should we regard those who are brethren and sisters of our Lord! Should we not be quick to recognize the claims of our divine relationship? Adopted into the family of God, should we not honor our Father and our kindred?"—*Ibid.*, p. 327.

Paul makes use of this larger concept of the Christian family when he treats Timothy as his "own son in the faith." 1 Timothy 1:2. An additional link between them was their knowledge of the Scriptures, which Timothy had known from a child and which Paul had studied diligently as a Pharisee, evidenced by his numerous quotations from the Old Testament. They differed, however, in that Paul was "an Hebrew of the Hebrews," "circumcised the eighth day" (Philippians 3:5), whereas Timothy was the son of a Greek father and a Jewish mother and was not circumcised until he joined with Paul in missionary work (Acts 16:1, 3). The two were knit together in the bonds of friendship and Christian brotherhood, the older man passing on his experience to the younger, thus multiplying himself in service.

Also listed in the Christian family are the names of some of Paul's companions in Rome: Eubulus, Pudens, Linus, Claudia, "and all the brethren." 2 Timothy 4:21. Here again we see the family picture; but this time some members are not named. They join that other anonymous group mentioned at the end of the "faith chapter," Hebrews 11. There, after briefly mentioning David and several others by name, the writer describes marvelous victories and apparent defeats, then continues, "and others. . . ." Hebrews 11:36. What eloquence in this brief allusion! Like the unknown soldier, they are "known but to God." But note: They *are* known to God! History does not record their names, but their work and witness made an important contribution to the continuity of the gospel message and are recorded in heaven.

In the secular world it is unfortunately quite common for individuals to perform a service and receive no credit. In a cricket match between England and Australia, one of the English players was unable for a short time to take his position in the field, so another man, not originally selected to the team, deputized for him. During the course of the game this man held a brilliant catch, but his name is now forgotten. In the record book his feat is simply listed as "c. sub . . ."; that is, "caught by a substitute whose name does not appear." Unnamed, but nevertheless most valuable.

In the spiritual world, the same is often true; but God's anonymous ones will be recognized in God's good time. "Among earth's inhabitants, scattered in every land, there are those who have not bowed the knee to Baal. Like the stars of heaven, which appear only at night, these faithful ones will shine forth when darkness covers the earth. . . . God has in reserve a firmament of chosen ones that will yet shine forth amidst the darkness, revealing clearly to an apostate world the transforming power of obedience to His law. Even now they are appearing in every nation . . . ; and in the hour of deepest apostasy, . . . these faithful ones . . . will 'shine as lights in the world.' Philippians 2:15. The darker the night, the more brilliantly will they shine."—*Prophets and Kings*, pp. 188, 189. It will be seen in the hereafter that Christians who are only names now, and even those who have received no mention at all, will have done exploits for God. They will be forever honored members of His great family.

A Young Missionary

One would expect a man of Paul's energy and ambition to find confinement in prison particularly galling. But no impatient frustration mars his final letter. He is sure that the work he has given his life to accomplish will flourish after he is gone and every goal will be more than realized.

His courage is explained by his confidence that Timothy will carry on. Paul found Timothy in Lystra and has spent years training him. Already, in spite of his youth, the young man is a successful church pastor, and Paul sees increasing success for him as time goes on.

It is clear, both from this epistle and from Paul's other writings, that the veteran worker was familiar with the work of other youth whose success has been recorded in Scripture.

Child training.

A human baby is the most helpless of all mammals and depends for years on its parents for sustenance and protection. During these early years the parents make a tremendous impact on their child. These are critical times which affect the future well-being of the small individual, for reactions to future external stimuli will follow patterns set by parental training. "In childhood and youth the character is most impressible. The power of self-control should then be acquired. By the fireside and at the family board influences are exerted whose results are as enduring as eternity. More than any natural endowment, the habits established in early years decide whether a man will be victorious or vanquished in

17

the battle of life. Youth is the sowing time. It determines the character of the harvest, for this life and for the life to come."—*The Desire of Ages*, p. 101.

This fact makes the work of mothers of great importance, as numerous examples in the Bible demonstrate. All parents would do well to ask themselves the question that the future father of Samson asked the angelic messenger: "How shall we order the child, and how shall we do unto him?" Judges 13:12.

In Samuel's early years, before he was transferred to the temple to live in Eli's home, he was guided wisely by his mother, Hannah. So successful was her training that he did not fall into the evil ways of Eli's sons, but sought solely to follow the Lord. "From the earliest dawn of intellect she [Hannah] had taught her son to love and reverence God and to regard himself as the Lord's. By every familiar object surrounding him she had sought to lead his thoughts up to the Creator."—*Patriarchs and Prophets*, p. 572.

Here is wisdom for mothers trying to train their children to fear God. It is a kind of parable-teaching method, leading from known and recognized objects to the unknown God who made them. It is evident that the mother herself must be a dedicated follower of the Lord so that she can speak with authority of spiritual things. "She may make straight paths for the feet of her children, through sunshine and shadow, to the glorious heights above. But it is only when she seeks, in her own life, to follow the teachings of Christ that the mother can hope to form the character of her children after the divine pattern."—*Ibid*.

What a reward accrues to the mother who sees her counsel and guidance bearing fruit for the Master after many years of patient care! Such came to the slave woman, Jochebed. Given only twelve years, she instilled in the young mind of her second son principles of truth and righteousness that withstood the corruption of the idolatrous court of Egypt. Jochebed achieved her goal by prayer, faith, and work. When Moses was but a baby only three months old, his "mother's earnest prayers had committed her child to the care of God; and angels, unseen, hovered above his lowly resting place. . . . She faithfully improved her opportunity to educate her child for God. . . . She endeavored to imbue his mind with the fear of God and the love of truth and justice, and earnestly prayed that he might be preserved from every corrupting influence." She "early taught him to bow down and pray to the living God, who alone could hear him and help him in every emergency."—*Patriarchs and Prophets*, pp. 243, 244.

Parents in the Christian era have a tremendous advantage over those who lived in Old Testament times. While many of the latter had access to the Law, the Prophets, and the Psalms, we have all that instruction and the New Testament besides. Well would it be if every mother would teach her children to commit the Scriptures to memory, so that in time of need these precious promises would flash back into the memory and guard against temptation and discouragement. The Holy Scriptures are, after all, the means by which we may gain a knowledge of God, of His will, of His plan for mankind, and of the gospel of salvation. A knowledge of them will therefore make us wise unto salvation, which ultimately is far more important than being wise in history or science or language study, interesting and necessary as these may be.

It should encourage every parent to know that today's children may learn the Scriptures just as the child Jesus learned them. We read that the Jews marveled at His wisdom, knowing that He had not been educated in rabbinical schools. They asked, "How knoweth this man letters, having never learned?" (John 7:15), meaning, of course, that He had not passed through their system of education. "Since He gained knowledge as we may do, His intimate acquaintance with the Scriptures shows how diligently His early years were given to the study of God's word."—*The Desire of Ages*, p. 70. How important it is, then, to train our children in the knowledge of the Bible, that they, like Timothy, may become wise unto salvation! The Word of God will stir the heart, and constant feeding on the Bread of Life will lead to conversion: "I have no greater joy than to hear that my children walk in truth." 3 John 4.

The call of God.

When God calls, a person must devote himself to service. The compelling urge reduces all else to insignificance. As Paul said, "Though I preach the gospel, I have nothing to glory of: for necessity is laid upon me; yea, woe is unto me, if I preach not the gospel!" 1 Corinthians 9:16.

The same dedication is seen in the great missionary to Africa, Dr. David Livingstone. Though qualified to practice medicine in easier lands, he dedicated his great capabilities to the Dark Continent. In the museum erected to his memory in Blantyre, his boyhood home in Scotland, is a stained-glass window on which is written: "I will place no value on anything I have or possess, except in relation to the kingdom of God." Spurred on by this resolve, he gave no thought to creature comforts, even to family life, but battled on, exploring the great continent and blunting the slave trade. Both these factors facilitated the proclamation of the gospel to those who had never heard the name of Christ. The success of his selfless dedication is reflected in the inscription on his tombstone in Westminster Abbey: "For thirty years his life was spent in an unwearied effort to evangelize the native races, to explore the undiscovered secrets, to abolish the desolating slave trade of Central Africa, where with his last words he wrote, 'May heaven's rich blessing come down on every one who will help to heal this open sore of the world.' 'Other sheep I have, which are not of this fold: them also I must bring, and they shall hear my voice.' John 10:16."

Timothy's call involved him too in a life away from home. When he left Lystra to join with Paul and Silas, it was the beginning of a pilgrim life.

It is possible to imagine that God is calling when, in fact, there is merely a personal desire to be a servant of the Lord. However, there can be no mistaking a divine call, for God sees to it that such a call is recognized also by others of His servants.

The devout centurion, Cornelius, a generous man of prayer, may well have wondered at the message the angel gave him. Apparently he had been praying for further guidance in the way of salvation. The angel told him to send for Peter. "He shall tell thee what thou oughtest to do," said the angel (Acts 10:6), so that "thou and all thy house shall be saved" (Acts 11:14). Could not the angel have revealed more? Evidently Peter could profit by the experience, so the Holy Spirit gave the apostle a vision while the servants of Cornelius were approaching his lodgings. The complementary visions confirmed the Lord's intervention, for the many details given to Cornelius rule out any possibility of coincidence.

It is interesting to note that the two different messages were given by the same heavenly messenger. "The angel, after his interview with Cornelius, went to Peter, in Joppa."—*The Acts of the Apostles*, p. 135.

We would do well to remember that God knows and, indeed, busies Himself with the most elementary affairs of earth. "The explicitness of these directions, in which was named even the occupation of the man with whom Peter was staying, shows that Heaven is acquainted with the history and business of men in every station of life. God is familiar with the experience and work of the humble laborer, as well as with that of the king upon his throne."—*Ibid.*, pp. 133, 134. There was a divine synchronization in the call to Cornelius and the vision to Peter so that the doubts of both were readily resolved.

Thus also in the conversion of Saul the persecutor. On the road to Damascus, the Lord said to him, "Arise, and go into the city, and it shall be told thee what thou must do." Acts 9:6. Temporarily blind, Saul was led to the house of Judas in Damascus, where he afflicted his soul and prayed. At the same time God spoke to Ananias, giving him the frightening assignment to visit the persecutor, "for, behold, he prayeth." Acts 9:11. All fears and doubts were resolved when Ananias obeyed. Saul was healed of his blindness and was baptized (Acts 22:10-16) by the man whom he had seen in vision (Acts 9:12). The double confirmation, with all the details involved, ensured that here too was a call from God. Thus we conclude that calls from the Lord are not merely fitful impressions, revealed to one individual alone. They are buttressed by divine interventions involving other parties too.

Furthermore God often chooses two men of differing, but complementary, talents to work together. Paul's rugged forthrightness was balanced by Timothy's readiness to find a gentler solution to problems. Timothy's shyness of approach was balanced by Paul's boldness. "Writers with a strong belief in divine providence have frequently said that God brought Luther and Melanchthon together to accomplish an otherwise impossible reformation."—Manschreck, *Melanchthon*, p. 55. This statement is preceded by a quotation from Luther's *Preface to the Commentary on Colossians*: "I am rough, boisterous, stormy, and altogether warlike. I am born to fight against innumerable monsters and devils. I must remove stumps and stones, cut away thistles, and thorns, and clear the wild forests; but Master Philip comes along softly and gently sowing and watering with joy, according to the gifts which God has abundantly bestowed upon him."—*Ibid.*, p. 54.

Hardship and success. 2 Timothy 2:3.

Success implies triumphing over obstacles. We would expect, therefore, that hardship would be a prerequisite to success. It would not produce it, certainly, but present circumstances in which an individual might overcome or be overcome. The goal of true education is achieved by directing students "to the sources of truth, to the vast fields opened for research in nature and revelation. Let them contemplate the great facts of duty and destiny, and the mind will expand and strengthen. Instead of educated weaklings, institutions of learning may send forth men strong to think and to act, men who are masters and not slaves of circumstance, men who possess breadth of mind, clearness of thought, and the courage of their convictions."—*Education*, pp. 17, 18.

Even in the secular world, the human spirit has always risen to a challenge. When Sir Ernest Shackleton planned his third visit to the South Polar regions, this time as leader of the Imperial Trans-Antarctic Expedition in 1914, he called for volunteers to complete the 27-man crew. He was inundated with applications, more than 5,000 in fact, including three from girls. One young man even stowed away at Buenos Aires when his ship, *Endurance*, left this last port of civilization.

The ocean cruise was by no means a joyride, but carried out in the spirit of the ship's name and Shackleton's family motto—"*Fortitudine Vincimus*, We conquer by endurance." The ship was crushed by pack ice, and the men camped on an ice floe until it was in danger of fragmenting. Then they braved the icy rigors of the world's worst seas in open boats, ultimately to land on bleak and inhospitable Elephant Island. Another hazardous journey faced Shackleton and five others before they reached South Georgia, but this brave captain brought all his men back alive, having endured untold hardships in spite of not achieving his prime objective.

Shackleton's sterling character was shown in his attitude toward unexpected hardships. The sun melts wax, but it bakes clay. The same external pressure and heat produce effects dependent on the quality of the material on which they act. *Circumstance* literally means "those things that stand around us." They have nothing to do with the strength or weakness that lies within us. Pressure may build up from without, but the will, rightly trained and exercised, may build up a greater pressure to resist. As someone has said, "What matters is not so much the size of the dog in the fight, but the size of the fight in the dog!"

Public opinion is a dangerous circumstance, for it is fickle. To be swayed by it one way or another is to allow oneself to be swept away by circumstance, caught in a current running rapidly in a direction one may not wish to go. The apostle Paul experienced the fickleness of public opinion, and, knowing its uncertainty, was not moved by it. On his first visit to Timothy's home city he miraculously healed a cripple. The heathen citizens were so impressed that they said, "The gods are come down to us in the likeness of men." Acts 14:11. But after listening to some dissident Jews, they quickly changed their minds, and, "having stoned Paul, drew him out of the city, supposing he had been dead." Verse 19.

Just as Paul was undeterred by this treatment, so was he not deceived by the opposite. When landing on Malta after shipwreck, he helped to gather sticks for a fire. A viper fastened on his hand, and the barbarians said, "No doubt this man is a murderer" (Acts 28:4) who though not drowned would certainly die of poisoning. But no harm came to the apostle, and the Maltese "changed their minds, and said that he was a god." Verse 6.

Rudyard Kipling expressed the same thought in "If"

If you can meet with Triumph and Disaster
And treat those two imposters just the same.

The attitude was prophesied of our Lord by Isaiah: "He shall not fail nor be discouraged." Isaiah 42:4. And Jesus was not discouraged, even though circumstances were so forbidding that many of His disciples left Him to return to their former occupations. Jesus set before Himself the goal of triumphing over every foe; and He, the Missionary sent from heaven to rescue the inhabitants of earth, faced hardship without flinching and gained success. External circumstances, disheartening or encouraging, did not deflect Him from His purpose. "He was never elated by applause, nor dejected by censure or disappointment. Amid the greatest opposition and the most cruel treatment, He was still of good courage."—*The Desire of Ages*, p. 330.

Jesus realized that His followers would face difficulties and that they must have inward strength, so He allowed them to come into problems that they might call upon inner resources to solve them. He multiplied Himself by training successors. Paul multiplied himself by training Silas and Timothy, Luke and Titus, and none of them found this earthly life a bed of roses.

Stephen was a monk in Mar Saba, a monastery overlooking the desolate country surrounding the Dead Sea. He wrote in a hymn translated by John Mason Neale:

> If I find Him, if I follow,
> What my portion here?
> "Many a sorrow, many a labor,
> Many a tear."
> —*The Church Hymnal*, no. 341

Is then the call to be Christ's servant worthwhile? Are the difficulties too great? Will the challenge fall on deaf ears? What testimony do our forebears give? Note the triumphant response in Stephen's hymn:

> Finding, following, keeping, struggling,
> Is He sure to bless?
> "Saints, apostles, prophets, martyrs,
> Answer, Yes."
> —*Ibid.*

"This charge I commit unto thee, son Timothy," "the same commit thou to faithful men, who shall be able to teach others also." 1 Timothy 1:18; 2 Timothy 2:2. So Paul helped to construct a portion of the endless chain that reaches from Jesus to the last disciple on earth.

God's Gifts

I do not know what procedures Roman law enforcers followed when admitting new prisoners. We know that current practice allows modern prisoners to take into their cells very few personal belongings and certainly no tools or instruments of a trade or profession beyond perhaps a pencil.

This prohibition must be among the most frustrating of all prison restrictions. Paul could have felt it keenly and chafed under it. But his last letter to Timothy reveals that he saw in the hands of every Christian tools that can be far more effective in building up God's church than hammers and saws could ever be, and many of them can be taken right into prison! Having a supply with him kept Paul encouraged.

These tools, in Paul's understanding, are the talents God has given everyone—to some, a few; to others, more. And a person's usefulness depends on what he does with them. Well used, some are effective even in prison. Neglected, however, they can be useless, even outside prison. Paul urges Timothy to "stir up the gift of God, which is in thee." 2 Timothy 1:6. Let's look at these God-given gifts and see why they cheered our famous prisoner.

All are gifted. 2 Timothy 1:6.

Among all the billions of people who have been born on our globe, there are no duplicates, not even among identical twins. We are all different, with our own peculiar characteristics and habits of life. Special gifts or talents mark us as different from others, even if they also have a talent we possess.

These gifts from God are bestowed in unequal measure at the outset. They increase or diminish, depending on our use or non-use of them. Things that we delight in doing, which may seem uninteresting or even distasteful to others, indicate our particular talents. Spending time using these gifts is not hard work even when we use them earning our daily bread. In this case we are well fitted for the task we are performing and will discharge our work satisfactorily, little realizing how fast time is passing. The converse is also true. Those whose work requires gifts they do not possess often become mere automatons, clock-watchers, finding little enjoyment in their compulsory working hours.

Talents are, however, not always immediately evident. Often an individual is not subjected to circumstances that help reveal a particular talent, and it lies hidden, unknown until the right stimulus or opportunity makes it manifest. Happy the man or woman whose early education opens a multitude of doors and a broad range of subjects, both academic and practical, to help reveal the special talents with which that person is gifted.

Everybody, without exception, has at least one talent; for example,

He couldn't sing and he couldn't play,
He couldn't speak and he couldn't pray.
He'd try to read, but break right down,
Then sadly grieve at smile or frown.
While some with talents ten begun,
He started out with only one.
"With this," he said, "I'll do my best,
And trust the Lord to do the rest."
His trembling hand and tearful eye
Gave forth a world of sympathy,
When all alone with one distressed,
He whispered words that calmed the breast,
And little children learned to know,
When grieved and troubled, where to go.
He loved the birds, the flowers, the trees,
And, loving him, his friends loved these.
His homely features lost each trace
Of homeliness, and in his face
There beamed a kind and tender light
That made surrounding features bright.
When illness came he smiled at fears

And bade his friends to dry their tears;
He said "Goodbye," and all confess
He made of life a grand success.
　　—Author Unknown

Some talents can still be developed late in life. It is no use bewailing lost opportunities, for while life is here, so is opportunity. In the formative period of American history, many men saw what could be done, but excused themselves on the ground of old age. Henry Wadsworth Longfellow answered that excuse in his fiftieth-anniversay poem for the graduation class of 1825:

It is too late! Ah, nothing is too late
Till the tired heart shall cease to palpitate.
Cato learned Greek at eighty; Sophocles
Wrote his grand Aedipus, and Simonides
Bore off the prize of verse from his compeers,
When each had numbered more than fourscore years;
And Theophrastus at fourscore and ten
Had but begun his "Characters of Men."
Chaucer at Woodstock, with the nightingales,
At sixty wrote the "Canterbury Tales."
Goethe at Weimar, toiling to the last,
Completed "Faust" when eighty years were past.
　　—*Morituri Salutamus*

A sound mind. 2 Timothy 1:7.

The two Gadarene demoniacs whom Jesus healed saw the kind of work the devils which had possessed them could do when they entered the herd of swine. The men were then in their right minds, and "their eyes beamed with intelligence."—*The Desire of Ages*, p. 338. They were now in full possession of their God-given faculties. But the chief men of the city who had chained them in the desert place, and who may have been the owners of the swine, were really no more sane than the two former demoniacs had been. Though their visitor was the Saviour of the world, "they besought him that he would depart out of their coasts." Matthew 8:34. What utter folly, sheer madness; clearly, they were not in their right minds. Dr. Luke continues the story with a happy ending, for the demoniacs, who were eager to stay with Jesus, were encouraged to "go home . . . and tell . . . how great things the

Lord hath done for thee." Mark 5:19. As a result of their witness, "when Jesus was returned, the people gladly received him." Luke 8:40. Obviously they had experienced a return of reason too!

The power of love.

Power is often envisaged as brute force, sledgehammer blows crushing everything that opposes. But the greater power of love is illustrated by the legendary argument between the wind and the sun. Noting a pedestrian wearing an overcoat, the wind challenged the sun to get the coat off. The wind began, and the man huddled more tightly within his overcoat. The wind blustered and blew. It stormed and raged, and the man buttoned himself up all the more securely. Acknowledging failure, the wind gave place to the sun. It shone its beams upon the man, who began to perspire. He undid the buttons and opened the coat. The sun increased its warmth. The man removed his coat and carried it over his arm. Benevolent beams of love and friendship are much more effective than unbridled force and compulsion.

Talents.

While we should be well-balanced and not extreme, there are certain aspects of our characters that reveal a special gift or ability. This is God-given, and we are responsible for using and developing it to the glory of the Giver. Ability in writing could lead to the writing of exciting novels which would earn their author a fortune. Composing music could result in the production of popular hits which would not uplift anyone but would perhaps entertain them, and at the same time bring in wealth for the composer.

Fanny Crosby had a gift for rhyming which she used to compose popular verse and secular songs with great success until she was in her early forties. This was acceptable work. But when William Bradbury, a Baptist choir director and organist, who published Sunday School songs, suggested that Fanny devote her talent to writing Christian songs, she agreed. She never wrote another secular song, but produced an enormous number of gospel songs during the last fifty years of her life, including "Blessed Assurance, Jesus Is Mine," "Jesus Is Tenderly Calling Today," "Take the World, But Give Me Jesus," "Pass Me Not, O Gentle

Saviour," "Jesus, Keep Me Near the Cross," to name only a few
of the many that are still bringing people closer to Jesus.

A similar experience happened to Will Lamartine Thompson.
At the age of forty, after tremendous success writing popular
songs that swept the United States, he decided to turn his talent
exclusively to gospel songs. One of his compositions, "Softly and
Tenderly Jesus Is Calling," was extensively used in the Moody-
Sankey revival meetings in Europe and North America and is still
greatly loved.

The gift of talents to human beings is God's way of doing His
work on earth. He could, and sometimes has, used angels; but
generally He invites men and women to share His work and experience the thrill of being God's helping hand. The world-renowned
violin maker who passed to his rest 250 years ago, and who has
left his name as the symbol of the world's finest violins, said of
himself: "If my hand slacked, I should rob God, since He is fullest
good, leaving a blank behind instead of violins. He could not make
Antonio Stradivari violins without Antonio."—Quoted in *The
Lighted Way*, by Milton E. Kern, p. 79.

Without wishing to imply that God's work cannot be done without man, but underlining the fact that God chooses man to use him
for His purpose, the poet expresses it thus:

> God has no hands but our hands
> To do His work today,
> He has no feet but our feet
> To lead men in His way,
> He has no tongues but our tongues
> To tell men how He died,
> He has no help but our help
> To bring them to His side.
>
> We are the only Bible
> The careless world will read,
> We are the sinner's gospel,
> We are the scoffer's creed.
> We are the Lord's last message,
> Given in deed and word,
> What if the type is crooked?
> What if the print is blurred?

What if our hands are busy
With other work than His?
What if our feet are walking
Where sin's allurement is?
What if our tongues are speaking
Of things His lips would spurn?
How can we hope to help Him
And hasten His return?
—*Annie Johnson Flint*

Misuse of talents.

Being merely busy, however, must not be confused with developing the gift that is within us. See 2 Timothy 1:6. Activity is not always useful or productive. Even converting someone does not justify boundless unprofitable activity, as our Lord made plain to the scribes and Pharisees: "Ye compass sea and land to make one proselyte and when he is made, ye make him two-fold more the child of hell than yourselves." Matthew 23:15.

We can be very busy doing wrong or doing nothing; or we can be very busy in the sense of being busybodies, very active with the tongue, but idle with the hands. There were such in Paul's day, as is evident by his remarks to the Thessalonians and to Timothy: "We hear that there are some which walk among you disorderly, working not at all, but are busybodies." 2 Thessalonians 3:11. They were busy yet idle as, "Withal they learn to be idle . . . and not only idle, but tattlers also and busybodies, speaking things which they ought not." 1 Timothy 5:13.

Being busy about the wrong things can be very dangerous, as exemplified by Ahab when he spared the life of Benhadad of Syria. An unnamed prophet said to Ahab: "A man turned aside, and brought a man unto me, and said, Keep this man: if by any means he be missing, then shall thy life be for his life, or else thou shalt pay a talent of silver. And as thy servant was busy here and there, he was gone. And the king of Israel said unto him, So shall thy judgment be; thyself hast decided it." 1 Kings 20:39, 40. King Ahab's judgment was the one made upon himself; but the significant point which we emphasize was that busyness did not excuse failure in a more important issue. Trifling about nonessentials is a waste of talent, and could be a waste of life too.

It is interesting to note that the parable of the talents and the parable of the pounds are both associated with the idea of waiting for our Lord's return. After the eschatological prophecy of Matthew 24, our Lord continued: "Then shall the kingdom of heaven be likened" (Matthew 25:1), which introduces the parable of the ten virgins, succeeded by a warning to "watch therefore" (verse 13). Then comes the story of the talents which are to be used in the waiting period. The story of the ten pounds given to ten servants was given specifically "because they thought that the kingdom of God should immediately appear." Luke 19:11. Here again is a waiting period, and at any time before the second advent there is this waiting period, one in which talents are not to be buried but exercised.

The possession of only one talent is no excuse for laziness. It can be multiplied just as were the two and the five talents. Better still, as in the parable in Luke, a single talent can be increased five times or ten times, depending on the efforts of the man who possesses it and not on the quantity of talents originally possessed.

Again, the Lord expects us to use what we have even though He can work miracles without us. In the miracle of the loaves and fishes, He used what man had to offer.

> He might have turned the stones to bread,
> Who once had made the water wine,
> Or called the manna down from heaven
> To show His power divine.
>
> But, "Give ye them to eat," He said,
> And took His servant's little store;
> Though scarce enough for one it seemed,
> He blessed and made it more.
>
> And so He let them share with Him
> His joy, His work of feeding men.
> And all they gave Him He returned
> A thousandfold again.
> —*Annie Johnson Flint*

How important little things are is shown in the sudden collapse of a huge silo in a health food company wholesale plant in Auckland, New Zealand. With a totally unexpected rushing sound, the steel sides of the silo, bearing the weight of tons of grain, burst open, spilling the precious wheat onto the ground. An insurance examination after the wheat had been removed indicated that the bolts specified for joining the metal sections were half an inch shorter—only half an inch—than required in the plan. They had been substituted by workmen who considered them to be near enough, and that it was not worth the delay in obtaining the bolts precisely specified.

Guarding the deposit.

In his short epistle, Jude, the brother of James, speaks of "the faith which was once delivered unto the saints." Verse 3. A body of Christian teaching, initiated by Christ and forming the basis of Christian belief, had been handed down, a tradition in the proper sense. Jude urged those who now followed in the Christian way to maintain this pure doctrine.

Paul, writing to the Romans, compared Jew and Gentile and pointed out that the Jews had advantages, the chief one being "that unto them were committed the oracles of God." Romans 3:2. God's law had been entrusted to them, but they had been unfaithful to their trust. They had misinterpreted God's message, and they had added to and subtracted from it until their human meddling had distorted God's Word. But the Author of the Word found others, notably Paul and Timothy, who would handle this treasure carefully and use it to the glory of God.

This treasure or deposit is not something inanimate or static, as is clearly shown in the parables. The kingdom of God is likened to a mustard seed. See Mark 4:31. The mustard seed was chosen not only because it was small, but also because it had life in it. Otherwise, a grain of sand would have been adequate for the parable. But the essence of the kingdom is that it has the potential for growth. The seed must not be stifled, rather watered and tended. God has committed this trust to His followers in the Christian church, and it is their responsibility to advance the kingdom of grace in the earth. God Himself will ensure that growth will ensue, for though there be opposition and sometimes apparent defeat, He has His hand upon His work, and "we can do nothing against the truth, but for the truth." 2 Corinthians 13:8. Christians have a mighty privilege, to be entrusted with God's message. "We were allowed of God to be put in trust with the gospel." 1 Thessalonians 2:4.

Paul compares the glorious gospel to a brilliant light dispelling the darkness of unbelief. Just as the Creator illuminated the "darkness" which "was upon the face of the deep" (Genesis 1:2), so He has shined the light of His gospel into darkened minds blinded by prejudice and self-will (2 Corinthians 4:4-6). The apostle goes on to describe this gift of God as a treasure which weak, puny humans possess in humble earthen vessels, lest the effulgent glory of the gospel transformation be attributed to the container rather than to the contents. "We have this treasure in earthen vessels, that the excellency of the power may be of God, and not of us." Verse 7. The gospel tradition is in safekeeping, for while it is transmitted by human agents who are imperfect, and sometimes even apostate and unfaithful, its ultimate repository is the Almighty Himself. He will cause His truth to multiply; and though death remove His servants, His Word "liveth and abideth for ever." 1 Peter 1:23.

Unashamed

Shame is what prison is all about. Society turns its back on prisoners, excluding them from their company as unworthy to be among decent, law-abiding people. Prisoners should be so ashamed they cry. Paul is in prison. He does not cry, for he is not ashamed; and he urges Timothy not to be ashamed of him. See 2 Timothy 1:8.

Two kinds of shame.

Shame is a God-given emotion, but it can be used to produce actions that are anything but Godlike. Satan has deformed it to evil ends. However, when we recognize that shame is God-given, we can utilize it to His glory. For example, shame punishes us for sins we commit, producing feelings of disgust and a desire not to repeat such errors. Although not sufficiently strong by itself to keep us in the right way, shame often motivates us to obtain help.

Shame is used by Satan as a means of persuading us not to do right. The sneers of others, the inferiority felt when we are alone in our beliefs, the pressure of the majority can induce such feelings of shame in our hearts that we bow to the pressure and violate principles we know to be true. Then true shame overwhelms us, and we face the dilemma of God-given shame at doing wrong in conflict with another shame at doing right, because we fear man and his taunts.

Shame has other aspects. If a person is innocent of a crime for which he is condemned, he may be despised by his fellows who heap shame on him for allegedly committing such a disgraceful act; but he himself has an internal feeling of innocence and pride, for he is not ashamed of his conduct, which has been correct.

There are experiences of which we, as Christians, should be ashamed. On the other hand, there are other experiences of which we should never be ashamed.

Unashamed of Christian friends in trouble.

In some countries today Christians are persecuted by torture, imprisonment, even death. We expect the practice to spread widely in the future. What will our emotions be when our friends are haled away to prison, reproached and scorned for their Christian life-style? That's when the principles we have embraced in times of peace and quietness will be put to the test. If we have decided in advance to remain true to Christ, our wills will be placed on the side of the powerful Holy Spirit, and in His strength we will conquer. However, if we rely only on the feelings of the moment, without prior firm convictions, we will probably fall prey to situation ethics and choose the course that seems easiest, making convenience instead of conscience the ground for our decision.

The classic case of such dallying, setting expediency before principle, is the example of King Herod, who vacillated between his lust for Herodias and his desire to hear John the Baptist preach. At first he showed some signs of strength, for he refused his adulterous companion's request to have John killed and went only so far as to have him jailed. See Mark 6:19, 20. For a while he leaned toward John and "heard him gladly." Verse 20. But the wily Herodias was too subtle for him. At her first opportunity she laid a fearful trap. When suddenly confronted with a dreadful dilemma, Herod wanted to avoid the shame of breaking a solemn promise before his guests. This would mean executing the prophet, a shameful betrayal of his responsibility to him. But to save the prophet would mean shame for himself before Herodias and his guests. The situation was of the devil's own making, and Herod wrote a shameful name in history. Our principles must be so firmly established that shame at violating them will help us always to choose the right path, even when confronted with dilemmas of frightening proportions.

This philosophy does not contradict Paul's well-known words: "I am made all things to all men" (1 Corinthians 9:22), for there he was explaining that his approaches to different people were different for the sole purpose "that I might by all means save some." His principles were firm as a rock, and no situation, dangerous as it might be, could in any way change his allegiance to Christ and the preaching of His gospel. His conduct was akin to advice later given by St. Ambrose to St. Augustine: "When in Rome, live as the Romans do; when elsewhere, live as they live elsewhere." In other words, in matters where principle is not at stake, adapt yourselves to the people among whom you live and whom you hope to influence for truth and right. However, in matters of principle, let no one shame you into deviating one iota from your fixed moral standards. If then our fellow members suffer shame or imprisonment or persecution of any kind, we must strengthen their faith and not desert them in their hour of need. We can refresh them as Onesiphorus refreshed Paul. See 2 Timothy 1:16.

Unashamed of suffering. 2 Timothy 1:8, 12.

Timothy was well aware that suffering was almost synonymous with discipleship, for his introduction to Paul had been to see him mercilessly stoned at Lystra and left for dead. "In this dark and trying hour the company of Lystrian believers . . . remained loyal and true. The unreasoning opposition and cruel persecution by their enemies served only to confirm the faith of these devoted brethren; and now, in the face of danger and scorn, they showed their loyalty by gathering sorrowfully about the form of him whom they believed to be dead. . . . Among those who had been converted at Lystra, and who were eye-witnesses of the sufferings of Paul, was . . . a young man named Timothy. When Paul was dragged out of the city, this youthful disciple was among the number who took their stand beside his apparently lifeless body and who saw him arise, bruised and covered with blood, but with praises upon his lips because he had been permitted to suffer for the sake of Christ."—*The Acts of the Apostles*, pp. 184, 185.

Far from dissuading Timothy from entering the ministry "the impression then made had deepened with the passing of time until he [Timothy] was convinced that it was his duty to give himself fully to the work of the ministry."—*Ibid.*, p. 202. Notice then that suffering endured by his colleagues or himself did not give him any shame. Rather it stimulated him to greater effort. "In Timothy Paul saw one who . . . was not appalled at the prospect of suffering and persecution."—*Ibid.*, p. 203.

Later in life Timothy was actually imprisoned, but this news comes to us simply from the happy report: "Know ye that our brother Timothy is set at liberty." Hebrews 13:23.

One of Satan's well-used tools is the shame that comes from mental suffering, when in a crowd of unbelievers one is afraid to show his colors. One may fear to say grace in a public restaurant, for example, lest he be thought odd or suffering from religious mania. We may be tempted to use coarse, even profane, language when in the company of those who delight in foul oaths. The shame of being ostracized can be greater than the shame of denying one's beliefs. An internal battle goes on in the heart, and victory goes to the one who reigns in the heart, whether the Lord Jesus Christ or Satan. Shame helps thus in self-analysis and reveals to us what we really are. What a valuable tool then is this emotion in psychoanalysis, aiding us in being on our guard in life's quandaries, preparing in times of freedom from stress so that we can make the right choices in times of difficulty.

Norman MacLeod (1812-1872), a minister of the church of Scotland, was one of the chaplains to Queen Victoria and a very powerful orator. In a lecture to a group of young men entitled "A Life Story" he related the experience of one of his college friends and concluded his talk with a poem he had written. Its recurring theme was "Trust in God, and do the right." He emphasized the importance of looking to God, for man is frail and changeable:

> Some will hate thee, some will love thee,
> Some will flatter, some will slight;
> Cease from man, and look above thee;
> Trust in God, and do the right.
>
> Simple rule and safest guiding,
> Inward peace and shining light,
> Star upon our path abiding;
> Trust in God, and do the right.
> —*The Church Hymnal*, no. 263

A young soldier promised his mother that he would read his New Testament every evening before retiring, but in camp he found that the other men in his unit were profane and godless. He feared to carry out his promise. But his conscience was quickened, and he resolved to read his Bible, come what might. Coarse laughter greeted him, and a boot came flying over. Ribald songs filled the air. The young man persisted, gaining strength the next night and the next. After a while other soldiers in the unit gained courage to admit that they too were Christians and were ready to follow his example. They supported him by taking new courage themselves to witness for Christ.

Unashamed of Christ. 2 Timothy 1:12.

Is it possible that a Christian can be ashamed of Christ? Though the idea is unthinkable, unfortunately it is true, and borne out even by men who later gave their lives for the cause of their Master. An outstanding example is the apostle Peter. With the other disciples he said, "Though I should die with thee, yet will I not deny thee. Likewise also said all the disciples." Matthew 26:35. Yet but a few hours later, in spite of Jesus' warning, Peter had failed three times, with cursing and swearing, saying, "I know not the man." Verse 74. Unlike Judas, he was filled with sorrow and shame that he had so betrayed his Master. His salvation lay in his immediate repentance, for "he went out, and wept bitterly." Verse 75.

The words of a mere boy, Joseph Grigg (c. 1720-1768), express the utter impossibility of being ashamed of our Saviour. His poem, revised somewhat, appears as number 152 in *The Church Hymnal*. Note this example of the many striking contrasts in the hymn:

> A mortal man ashamed of Thee?
> Ashamed of Thee whom angels praise:
> Ashamed of Jesus! just as soon
> Let midnight be ashamed of noon; . . . sooner far
>
> Let evening blush to own a star.

Then comes the change from shame to boasting, pride in its proper sense:

>   . . . I boast a Saviour slain;
>   And O, may this my glory be,
>   That Christ is not ashamed of me!

The opposite emotion to shame is glory and humble pride, just as Jesus "endured the cross, despising the shame" and "endured such contradiction of sinners against himself." Hebrews 12:2, 3. He submitted to a most ignominious death, but in so doing exalted the symbol of shame. The cross is a prominent feature of the flags of many western European countries because of their Christian association. The Red Cross too, with the Swiss flag in reversed colors, stands for help in time of war to those who are sick or wounded or taken prisoner. Red Cross workers are granted immunity from attack as they carry out their humanitarian work. So we get the paradox of a shameful thing becoming a glorious thing. Now, instead of being ashamed of the cross which was "unto the Jews a stumblingblock, and unto the Greeks foolishness" (1 Corinthians 1:23), Christians proudly display it on their churches and around their necks.

Sir John Bowring wrote in 1825 with words now engraved on his tombstone: "In the cross of Christ I glory," and

> Bane and blessing, pain and pleasure,
> By the cross are sanctified.
> —*The Church Hymnal*, no. 125

Because Jesus "hid not his face from shame and spitting" (Isaiah 50:6), the shameful cross has become a symbol of glory.

The change has come about simply because of our Lord's life here on earth. Everything He touched became a blessing. Reproach for Christ's sake became honor. Martyrdom because of belief in Christ became a noble way to die. Disappointment, loss, contempt were not regarded by Christians as evils. They "took joyfully the spoiling of [their] goods," knowing they had treasure in heaven, "a better and an enduring substance." Hebrews 10:34. Their outlook on temporal things was conditioned by their uplook toward heavenly things.

Belief and trust in a Person rather than in a creed ensures that shame will not cause a believer to be untrue to principle. The sentiments of the Christians who were addressed in the epistle to the

Hebrews are poetically expressed in the hymn written by Elizabeth C. Clephane, "Beneath the Cross of Jesus":

> Content to let the world go by,
> To know no gain nor loss,
> My sinful self my only shame,
> My glory all the cross.
> —*The Church Hymnal*, no. 280

Ashamed of sin. 2 Timothy 2:19.

As we have just read in Miss Clephane's hymn, it is our sinful selves of which we must be ashamed; ashamed today, that is. We must not wait for the last day when the secrets of all hearts will be revealed, and some who sleep "in the dust of the earth shall awake . . . to shame and everlasting contempt." Daniel 12:2. Sin is a monster which appears attractive at first, but when we see it for what it really is, it is abhorrent. Eve in the Garden of Eden was perfectly safe from the serpent's wiles when she was away from the tree of knowledge of good and evil, for Satan "was not to follow them with continual temptations; he could have access to them only at the forbidden tree. Should they attempt to investigate its nature, they would be exposed to his wiles."—*Patriarchs and Prophets*, p. 53. It is obvious then that to wander into areas of temptation is to place ourselves in the net of one who is far more cunning than we.

This thought was evidently uppermost in Joseph's mind when he was tempted in the house of Potiphar. As a slave and a foreigner, he could not move out of his master's house, which would have been the simplest way to avoid the machinations and vile suggestions of Potiphar's wife. But he did the next best thing. "He hearkened not unto her . . . or to be with her." Genesis 39:10. In spite of this rebuff, the wicked woman watched for an opportunity when there were no other servants in the house. Trapped, but not by his fault, Joseph ran out of the house, keeping his conscience clear and his body unsullied. Even though he was subsequently imprisoned on the lying word of his mistress, yet in his incarceration, his action was exonerated. "The Lord was with him, and that which he did, the Lord made it to prosper." Genesis 39:23.

A little boy wandered to and fro in front of a grocer's display of juicy-looking apples. Back and forth he went, looking this way and that, obviously waiting for a chance to secrete one of the apples and be off. The proprietor noticed him and called out: "Ah, you are trying to steal my apples, aren't you?"

"No," came the reply. "I'm trying not to!"

"Then," said the proprietor, "be off with you as fast as you can."

If the lad really was trying not to steal, his obvious course was to run away from the fruit as fast and as far as his legs could carry him.

Our lingering at the place of temptation tempts Satan to tempt us. God's saints have not always set a good example in this respect. For example, David's adultery with Bathsheba evidently caused him shame, which he endeavored to hide by having Uriah killed. This caused even worse shame. But when rebuked by Nathan the prophet, David finally came to his senses and was thoroughly ashamed of his grievous sins. His sincere, spontaneous confession, "I have sinned against the Lord" (2 Samuel 12:13), and his penitential psalm, number 51, show how deeply ashamed he was at having sunk so low. His "broken and . . . contrite heart" (Psalm 51:17) and his open confession endeared him to the One who is willing to forgive. See Isaiah 57:15.

Before "the battle of that great day of God Almighty" (Revelation 16:14), the warning is given to watch and to keep one's garments, lest losing the garment of Christ's righteousness (see Revelation 19:8) a former Christian be naked, "and they see his shame" (Revelation 16:15). It is clear that those who are ashamed of having sinned will experience the opposite emotion—glory in the power of Christ to cover their sins and to grant them the power to overcome sin.

Our life is a life of denial. Either we deny self or we deny Christ; we own Christ, or we disown Him. There is no middle course. Our Lord's words about His being ashamed of those who are ashamed of Him (see Mark 8:38) were spoken as part of a sermon in which He had said that anyone who wanted to be His disciple must "deny himself, and take up his cross, and follow" (verse 34).

Paul's ringing testimony, "I am not ashamed" (2 Timothy 1:12) made a profound impression on Isaac Watts, a member of the Congregational or Independent Church which was despised and persecuted. His father was imprisoned for a time because he was a Dissenter. Isaac followed his father's religion nevertheless, and it began to flourish after restrictions imposed by the Act of Uniformity (1662) were removed. Isaac gave his testimony in his hymn published in 1707:

> I'm not ashamed to own my Lord,
> Or to defend His cause;
> Maintain the honour of His Word,
> The glory of His cross.
> Jesus, my God, I know His name—
> His name is all my trust:
> Nor will He put my soul to shame,
> Nor let my hope be lost.
> —*The Advent Hymnal (Revised)*, no. 643

What a glorious welcome that will be when the Lord greets His beloved with the words: "Come, ye blessed of my Father" (Matthew 25:34), a vivid and fearsome contrast to the words spoken to those who have been ashamed of Him: "Depart from me, ye cursed" (verse 41). As the unnamed prophet of Israel said to the unfaithful Eli: "Them that honour me I will honour, and they that despise me shall be lightly esteemed" (1 Samuel 2:30), a solemn message from the Lord of hosts.

Called According to Grace

Many a Christian, when things go wrong and his world starts falling around him, either blames God for bringing the changes or charges God with losing control. Both attitudes are discouraging. Paul found great comfort in believing that God had called him "according to his own purpose and grace" (2 Timothy 1:9) and that it was God's will that every event of his life would contribute to his ultimate success (see Romans 8:28). This attitude helped keep him buoyant and cheerful.

God's will. 2 Timothy 1:9.

God who created mankind knows what sort of creature man is. He knows the devil too, for He also created him. He is well acquainted with the continual warfare Satan wages for the capture of man's mind. He knows that some will come off victorious, through divine power, and that others will become the sport of Satan and join him in everlasting destruction.

The unscriptural doctrine of predestination claims that God arbitrarily marks some human beings for destruction and others for salvation, whatever their life on earth may be. We can be certain that God has not foreordained anyone to eternal death, for "God so loved the world, that he gave his only begotten Son, that *whosoever* believeth in him should not perish, but have everlasting life." John 3:16, emphasis supplied. That word *whosoever* opens the gate of mercy wide and disproves the dreadful teaching of predestination. Charles Wesley combated the idea vigorously in some of his hymns, for example:

Oh, for a trumpet voice,
On *all* the world to call!
To bid their hearts rejoice
In Him who died for *all*!
For *all* my Lord was crucified;
For *all*, for *all* my Saviour died!
—*The New Advent Hymnal*, no. 69, emphasis supplied

It was this good news that the disciples were asked to "teach," not to a limited, predestined audience, but to "*all* nations." Matthew 28:19. "Go ye into *all* the world," Jesus said. "Preach the gospel to *every* creature." Mark 16:15, emphasis supplied. The gospel is universal, but it does not necessarily bring universal salvation. In his hymn, "Would Jesus Have the Sinner Die?" Wesley emphasized that God's gift of His Son is for everyone:

Oh let Thy love my heart constrain.
Thy love for *every* sinner free,
That *every* fallen soul of man
May taste the grace that found out me;
That *all mankind* with me may prove
Thy sovereign everlasting love.
—*The New Advent Hymnal*, no. 117, emphasis supplied.

Paul had no doubt about the subject, for he wrote of Christ "that he died for all" (2 Corinthians 5:15), using this as an established fact to prove that we are all dead in trespasses and sins. When God proceeds with the work of final judgment, destroying unrepentant sinners, He calls it "his strange work, his strange act." Isaiah 28:21.

Man's choice.

It is man himself who brings about his own destruction by rejecting God's gracious pardon and following his own selfish way instead. Satan has injected his poison into man's intellectual ideas. The tendency of the natural man is to consider himself independent, to follow his own course of action. This makes him an easy prey to Satan's devices. It is illustrated in the lives of the two Sauls.

The Old Testament Saul was actually "turned into another man," for "God gave him another heart." 1 Samuel 10:6, 9. Alas, he soon reverted to his original state. He directly disobeyed God's explicit instructions regarding Amalek. Yet, in his self-inflicted blindness, he boasted, "I have performed the commandment of the Lord." 1 Samuel 15:13. Samuel described Saul's actions as "rebellion," which he said was the same as "the sin of witchcraft." And "stubbornness," he added, "is as iniquity and idolatry." Verse 23. It had been God's purpose to save Saul, but Saul himself was the stumbling block to his own salvation.

Saul of the New Testament, Saul of Tarsus, was, if anything, even more opinionated than his namesake. His own testimony later was, "I verily thought with myself, that I ought to do many things contrary to the name of Jesus of Nazareth. Which things I also did . . . being exceedingly mad against them." Acts 26:9-11. But the voice on the Damascus road brought him to his senses, and he "was not disobedient unto the heavenly vision." Verse 19. Saul the king had started on the heights, full of promise, but plunged to the depths. Saul the Pharisee, from being "less than the least" (Ephesians 3:8) ascended to heights that have been scaled by few others. Under trial, Saul the king failed and "brought dishonor upon the service of God."—*Patriarchs and Prophets*, p. 627. His victory over the Amalekites "served to rekindle the pride of heart that was his greatest peril."—*Ibid.*, p. 629. "Saul acknowledged his guilt, which he had before stubbornly denied; but he still persisted in casting blame upon the people. . . . It was not sorrow for sin, but fear of its penalty, that actuated the king."—*Ibid.*, p. 631.

When Saul the Pharisee, suffering physical blindness, realized his spiritual blindness he stopped trusting himself and began to put his faith in the Lord. "What wilt *thou* have me to do?" (Acts 9:6, emphasis supplied) was his cry from that moment on until the end of his life. His expression "less than the least," is a kind of comparative superlative, for he used the Greek word for "least" and then the usual grammatical construction for making a comparative. If there were such an English word in existence, it would be "leaster," which serves only to emphasize the value Paul put upon himself when he compared himself with Christ.

Today our lives must be guided by this principle of self-renunciation and of obedience to Christ. "If we consent, He will so identify Himself with our thoughts and aims, so blend our hearts and minds into conformity to His will, that when obeying Him we shall be but carrying out our own impulses. The will, refined and sanctified, will find its highest delight in doing His service."—*The Desire of Ages*, p. 668. Listen to this wonderful promise for those who copy this pattern of serving and communing with God: "Those who decide to do nothing in any line that will displease God, will know, after presenting their case before Him, just what course to pursue. And they will receive not only wisdom, but strength."—*Ibid*.

Called and chosen.

Two parables end with the solemn words: "Many are called, but few are chosen." See Matthew 22:14 and Matthew 20:16. The first parable describes the marriage of the king's son. We are told that one guest presumed to attend without wearing the special wedding garment the king had provided. Evidently he had entered the banquet hall on his own terms, because, when challenged by the king, he was speechless. He had no excuse. The garment was free, but he had despised it. Admission was by grace, not by self-estimation. This self-assured individual was cast out, barred from participating in the bridal feast.

The other parable teaches the same lesson, and its conclusion is summarized similarly. The laborers first hired were given a definite contract. Those who were hired at the third, sixth, and eleventh hours were simply told that they would receive "whatsoever is right." Matthew 20:4. At day's end, each received exactly the same amount, which caused grumbling among those who had worked longer than the others. The reward was evidently of grace. It was not calculated by the hours worked. Those who thought they had earned something were told, "Go thy way" (verse 14)—a curt dismissal to all who imagine they are saved by works and not by grace. It appears that such are called, but are not later chosen. How often God works to show that man's might accomplishes little, and is, in comparison with the power of God, precisely nothing! Take another look at His use of Jonathan and his armorbearer to defeat the host of the Philistines. See 1 Samuel 14:1-16. Even more outstanding was His destruction of

Sennacherib's Assyrian army outside the walls of Jerusalem. See Isaiah 37:35, 36.

An even more interesting example of being called, and either chosen or not chosen, is given us in the progressive reduction of Gideon's army. At the first call for volunteers, 32,000 men answered. See Judges 6:34. But many were in heart "fearful and afraid" and took the first opportunity to change their minds; 22,000 went home. See Judges 7:3. Even then, most of the remaining 10,000 were not fit for the task. Finally only a few, 300 men, were chosen. Verses 6-8.

It is significant that the apostle John described those who gain the victory with the Lamb as "called, and chosen, and faithful." Revelation 17:14. They are in heaven because of faith, not works. Adam and Eve in the Garden of Eden, "naked and ashamed. . . . tried to supply the place of the heavenly garments by sewing together fig-leaves for a covering." But "nothing can man devise to supply the place of the lost robe of innocence. . . . This robe, woven in the loom of heaven, has in it not one thread of human devising. Christ in His humanity wrought out a perfect character, and this character He offers to impart to us."—*Christ's Object Lessons*, p. 311.

The man at the feast was called but was not also chosen, because he was like many today who "think that they are good enough in themselves, and they rest upon their own merits instead of trusting in Christ."—*Ibid*., p. 315.

"The householder's dealing with the workers in his vineyard represents God's dealing with the human family. It is contrary to the customs that prevail among men. In worldly business, compensation is given according to the work accomplished. The laborer expects to be paid only that which he earns." God's "reward is given, not according to our merit, but according to His own purpose."—*Ibid*., pp. 396, 397.

It is not the amount of time that we labor that makes us acceptable to God, but the spirit in which we do the work. The call is to serve; and the manner of service, not its mere length, determines whether God can choose those He has invited to the feast or to His work in His vineyard. "Heaven's golden gate opens not to the self-exalted. It is not lifted up to the proud in spirit. But the everlasting portals will open wide to the trembling touch of a little child. Blessed will be the recompense of grace to those who have wrought for God in the simplicity of faith and love."—*Ibid.*, p. 404.

The life-work.
While our thoughts may be in heaven, our feet are still on earth. We are "fellow-citizens with the saints, and of the household of God." Ephesians 2:19. The writer of these words realized that the city of which the saints are citizens had not been established on earth. Until it is, the saints must provide for their earthly sustenance. Paul, himself a spiritual giant, was also eminently practical. As a preacher, he could justifiably have lived on the support given by his flock, as he told the Corinthians. See 1 Corinthians 9:7-14. But he did not avail himself of this right. He had learned a trade, and he exercised this craft in Corinth with his hosts, Aquila and Priscilla, who also were tentmakers. Each person coming to adulthood must earn his living in some way or another, a principle also enunciated by the apostle: "If any would not work, neither should he eat." 2 Thessalonians 3:10.

While the choice of an occupation may seem a mundane matter, yet to the child of God it is of vital importance. Any occupation should be considered in the light of God's appointment. If God has called us and chosen us, this is not the end of His intervention on our behalf. He wants us to serve Him as we perform our daily duties. What a responsibility for teachers of children and youth as they seek to instill in their minds the ambition to serve the Lord, whether as manual workers, clerical workers, nurses, doctors, teachers, accountants, farmers, engineers, or mothers. No work is drudgery when one realizes that every moment he is influencing his workmates for good or ill. His attitudes under stress or disappointment, his reactions to unpleasant circumstances, all have a bearing on the witness which the Christian gives to the world.

A medical missionary in a difficult foreign field hoped that his son would follow in his footsteps. But no, the son wanted to be a printer! Undismayed, the father said: "Then be the best printer there is, my boy." Spurred on by this encouragement, the son lifted his sights beyond the routine mechanical work of a printing house. He became an expert not only at operating a press, but also in lay-out, composition, advertising, sales, and management— skills which propelled him ultimately to one of the most responsible positions in the land. But more. Throughout his career he remained true to the highest ideals; namely, to serve the church and be a faithful witness of God. In time he was ordained a local elder of the church. He and his family are looked up to as noble examples of God's leading in the choice of an occupation.

Another good example comes to mind of a youth who was blessed with both high intelligence and a large measure of humility. Following in the footsteps of his parents, he became a member of the church. He employed his talents efficiently and became a consultant physician. Noted among his fellow physicians as an expert in his field, he is also known widely for his consistent practice of Christian principles. He now serves as a deacon in the Seventh-day Adventist church and is bringing up his family to follow the Lord. He earns his living, but he is living a full, abundant life, because it is geared to God's service. He is not employed by the church, but he gives and witnesses, helping the church reach out to others. His choice is plainly God's choice for him, and he is faithful after being called and chosen.

Countless other examples could be cited of such Christians, who, like William Carey, dedicated their lives to the spreading of the gospel. Carey "cobbled shoes to pay expenses." At age 31, he was the prime mover in the founding of the Baptist Missionary Society and later became a marvelously successful missionary in India.

Sanctified service.

Our means of livelihood must always be chosen in view of our citizenship in heaven. This will permit God to carry out the essential work of sanctification. All His saints are really priests of God who render offerings, not indeed of bulls and goats, but of holy lives, living for Christ, which is perhaps more difficult than dying for Him.

We are to be preachers of the Word of God, even though we may never stand in the pulpit, and indeed may tremble at appearing before a congregation to make a simple announcement. But preachers we all are, and the godly witness of a sanctified life is one of the most powerful arguments for Christianity. Being preachers, we must know the Word which we preach. Timothy was a diligent student of the Holy Scriptures, and we should follow his example.

The psalmist gave the secret of consistent witnessing when he said, "Thy word have I hid in mine heart, that I might not sin against thee." Psalm 119:11. This is the way to increase faith, for "faith cometh by hearing, and hearing by the word of God." Romans 10:17. It is the next step after being called and chosen, as we have seen; for those who are found in the victorious army of the Lamb "are called, and chosen, and faithful." Revelation 17:14.

When God appoints a man to a task, that task becomes no longer commonplace. Being a doorkeeper in the house of the Lord is different from being a porter in a five-star hotel.

The story is told of a missionary who had spent years in a foreign country. He had learned the customs of the country, spoke several of the local dialects, and was not regarded by the inhabitants as a foreigner, for he identified so much with them. A business firm looking for a representative to serve them in this same country approached this missionary, offering a salary far above the denominational wage. Without any hesitation, he declined. The principals instructed their man to double the offer, but this too was refused. A third and even higher salary was suggested and again turned down.

"What is the matter?" asked the puzzled negotiator. "Isn't the salary big enough?"

"Why, certainly," the missionary replied. "The salary is fabulous, but your job is too small."

Would that we all might take this view of God's service!

The Master set us a pattern for our daily toil. When He was twelve years of age He posed the rhetorical question: "Wist ye not that I must be about my Father's business?" Luke 2:47. We assume that this implied that He was teaching the doctors of the law things that they were unaware of, pointing to a different conception of the Messiah and so preparing them for His own ministry in later years. The hidden years at Nazareth seem at first sight to be wasted, for Christ made no effort to announce Himself as the

Messiah. He labored faithfully in His father's business in the carpenter's shop and was identified as the carpenter's son. See Matthew 13:55. After His foster father's death He carried on the business and was recognized as the carpenter. See Mark 6:3. Those eighteen years were testing years, for His workmanship was a testimony to His honesty, His thoroughness, His punctuality.

"His trade was significant. He had come into the world as the character-builder, and as such all His work was perfect. Into all His secular labor He brought the same perfection as into the characters He was transforming by His divine power. He is our pattern. . . . Indolent, careless habits, indulged in secular work, will be brought into the religious life, and will unfit one to do any efficient service for God."—*Christ's Object Lessons*, p. 345.

"Religion and business are not two separate things; they are one. Bible religion is to be interwoven with all we do or say. Divine and human agencies are to combine in temporal as well as in spiritual achievements."—*Ibid.*, p. 349. "Because they are not connected with some directly religious work, many feel that their lives are useless; that they are doing nothing for the advancement of God's kingdom. But this is a mistake. If their work is that which some one must do, they should not accuse themselves of uselessness in the great household of God."—*Ibid.*, p. 359. "This is true sanctification; for sanctification consists in the cheerful performance of daily duties in perfect obedience to the will of God."—*Ibid.*, p. 360.

Soldier, Athlete, Farmer

One of the most significant reasons why our prisoner did not give way to tearful self-pity was that he *expected* to suffer. The modern concept that Christianity is a shortcut to easy problem-solving was totally foreign to him. We find him writing to Timothy that a Christian is like an athlete straining to prepare for a race, or like a farmer working hard to plow and plant and waiting patiently to reap. Even more appropriately for his present situation is his simile of a soldier, obeying without complaint and accepting the difficulties of the battlefield as necessary steps to victory.

Characteristics of a good soldier.

Obedience. We think of Joshua as the good soldier of the Lord, for although described as "Moses' minister" (Joshua 1:1), it was he who led the conquest of Canaan.

He recognized that he was under the command of a greater One and owed Him implicit obedience. This was shown after the Israelites crossed Jordan and came to the first formidable obstacle to their progress, the heavily fortified city of Jericho.

To conquer this city was Joshua's first task, but before tackling it, "he sought an assurance of divine guidance, and it was granted him. Withdrawing from the encampment to meditate and to pray that the God of Israel would go before his people, he beheld an armed warrior, of lofty stature and commanding presence."—*Patriarchs and Prophets*, p. 487. On learning that this was Christ, Joshua heard His instructions and obeyed them to the letter. See Joshua 5:13 to 6:5.

Obedience is expected of a soldier. In the disastrous charge of the Light Brigade against the Russian gunners in the Crimean War, it appears that the objective was mistaken. Lord Cardigan's order to charge sent those gallant men and their horses into a narrow valley guarded strongly by the enemy. They were, as Tennyson put it, charging

> Into the jaws of death,
> Into the mouth of Hell.

But they had been ordered to go, and though

> Some one had blundered:
> Theirs not to make reply,
> Theirs not to reason why,
> Theirs but to do and die.
> —"The Charge of the Light Brigade"

Obedience does sometimes lead to loss of life. John the Baptist gave us an outstanding example. He was a bold proclaimer of truth. In exposing the sins of his age, he came into conflict with Herod and, more seriously and dangerously, with Herodias. The latter, "would have killed him; but she could not." Mark 6:19. The prophet forfeited his life because of his soldierlike obedience to principle and truth.

Determination. The direction taken by a soldier is "forward." While retreat or strategic withdrawal may sometimes be a tactical necessity, the final objective is always "forward," no matter what difficulties loom ahead. It was so at the Red Sea for the fleeing Israelites.

The pillar of cloud seemed to have directed them wrongly. A mountain blocked their way southward, the sea posed an impassable barrier in front, and the Egyptian army's spears and swords glinted in the setting sun behind them. The people thought themselves doomed to perish in the desert or to be returned to slavery. In that desperate situation the word of the divine Captain was, "Speak unto the children of Israel, that they go forward." Exodus 14:15.

Forty years later another generation saw their entry into the promised land blocked by the overflowing Jordan. This time the forward advance required more faith. The priests must first step into the river before the river ceased to flow.

Even in retreat there must still be determination not to give in, as is well illustrated by Napoleon's frustrated army, unable to capture Moscow and now forced to turn back across harsh, desolate country in the biting winter. Those who soldiered on avoided frostbite, exposure, and certain death, and returned to their homeland, unsuccessful, but ready to fight again for their emperor.

So we must not expect our Christian warfare to be a bed of roses with no disappointments, defeats, or discouragements. The mettle of our determination to follow Christ to the end will be shown in our attitude to unexpected disasters. As Annie Johnson Flint expressed it:

> God hath not promised skies always blue,
> Flower-strewn pathways all our life through;
> God hath not promised sun without rain,
> Joy without sorrow, peace without pain.
> But God hath promised strength for the day,
> Rest for the labor, light for the way,
> Grace for the trials, help from above,
> Unfailing sympathy, undying love.

Her poem is a fitting description of her own life. She was orphaned at six, and her adoptive parents died when she was twenty-three. When she was twenty she contracted arthritis, and five years later was unable to walk.

Our watchword must be, "Onward, Christian soldiers! marching as to war." We belong to a church of which we can sing:

> Gates of hell can never
> 'Gainst that church prevail;
> We have Christ's own promise,
> That can never fail.
> —Sabine Baring-Gould, *The Church Hymnal*, no. 360

Dedication. The word *dedicate* comes from a Latin word *dedicare* which primarily means to "declare." Dedication then is a solemn declaration of intent. Paul declared, "This one thing I do." Philippians 3:13. His whole life was governed by his ultimate goal, "the prize of the high calling of God in Christ Jesus." Verse 14. He wrote to the church at Corinth, "Necessity is laid upon me; yea, woe is me, if I preach not the gospel!" 1 Corinthians 9:16. At his conversion he dedicated his life to building up the church he had formerly tried to tear down. Everything he did after that served to carry out this declaration of his intentions, and so continued until his martyrdom.

Dedication is a lifetime act. When a building such as a church is dedicated to God, the dedication does not end with the official ceremony. The sanctuary belongs to God as long as it stands, and so with the life. Dedication is not a spasmodic, temporary decision. It is a commitment to serve God all our days. "There is no discharge in that war." Ecclesiastes 8:8.

We live in the land of the dying. Death has passed upon all men, for all have come under the curse of sin. There is no escape from this curse save by the grace of our Lord Jesus Christ, who conquered in the fight and has opened for us a way through the grave. We have only one life in which to prepare for eternity, and the dedication of this life to the Lord is part of our duty as obedient, determined Christian soldiers.

Honesty. The parable of the sower is thought to be a simple one, and so it is, now that Jesus has interpreted it for us. But how profound it is! It reveals the condition of our hearts. No psychological examination opens ourselves to ourselves more than does this parable, especially as we have three versions of the story, each with some unique feature. Luke's account explains that the good-ground hearers are "they, which in an honest and good heart," hear and keep the word. Luke 8:15.

An honest heart is rare! Jeremiah knew that "the heart is deceitful above all things, and desperately wicked: who can know it?" Jeremiah 17:9. We are our own greatest enemy, for while we condemn errors we see in other people's conduct, we excuse ourselves for doing the same things. In doing this we are not honest. We deceive ourselves when we refuse to admit our errors and weaknesses. We should not blame the difficulties we encounter; they do not cause us to make mistakes, they merely reveal how weak we are.

Areas of weakness are present with us in good times but may be hidden while we are free from temptation. Our Lord once described a man from whom an evil spirit had been cast out. In Matthew 12:43-45 He said that the inner dwelling of that man's heart was made pure and clean, but there was no safety in that alone. Ultimately this man became the abode of seven other evil spirits, each more wicked than the original, so that the latter condition of this wretched man was not only eight times worse, but more depraved than that. The vacuum created by the expulsion of the evil spirit must be immediately filled with the abiding presence of the Holy Spirit. Otherwise we offer an open invitation to the devil to retake our heart and make it a stronger citadel for him than it was previously.

In the particular context of Paul's reference to living honestly and striving lawfully (see 2 Timothy 2:5), he is amplifying his former statement about not being entangled with things that would distract him from his duties as a soldier. Verse 4. Soldiers of Christ will follow the instruction given in the Sermon on the Mount: "If therefore thine eye be single, thy whole body shall be full of light." Matthew 6:22. The next verse says, "No man can serve two masters." Service and dedication to God require us to be transparently honest with ourselves, asking the Lord to give us discerning hearts.

Weapons. A soldier has certain weapons that are indispensable, specified in Ephesians 6:13-17. Let it be noted that these weapons are all spiritual, as indeed were those with which David slew Goliath. Certainly David did take some physical weapons—a staff, a sling, and five carefully chosen smooth stones. See 1 Samuel 17:40. But when the crisis came, notice David's words: "Thou comest to me with a sword, and with a spear, and with a shield." Verse 45. He might have added, "I come to thee with three weapons also." But faith was his dominant weapon, exceeding even his developed skill. No doubt, like the Benjamites who lived nearby, he could aim a stone "at an hair breadth, and not miss." Judges 20:16. But David's words were, "I come to thee in the name of the Lord of hosts, the God of the armies of Israel, whom thou hast defied," and "all this assembly shall know that the Lord saveth not with sword and spear." Verses 45-47. "When the servants of Christ take the shield of faith for their defense, and the sword of the Spirit for war, there is danger in the enemy's camp."—*Testimonies for the Church*, vol. 1, p. 407. "It is not safe for us, when going into battle, to cast away our weapons. It is then that we need to be equipped with the whole armor of God. Every piece is essential."—*Ibid.*, vol. 7, p. 190. "Let us be shod with the gospel shoes, ready to march at a moment's notice."—*Ibid.*, vol. 9, p. 48.

A soldier's march to victory will be hindered if his loins are not girded. Ours must be girded about with truth. Truth can have two meanings, and both are involved: not uttering falsehoods, and the Word of God along with its derived doctrines as opposed to the traditions of men.

Soldiers with ungirded loins are in danger of tripping, like contestants in a sack race! Untruth destroys itself, but honesty brings its own rewards. "He who utters untruths sells his soul in a cheap market. His falsehoods may seem to serve in emergencies; he may thus seem to make business advancement that he could not gain by fair dealing; but he finally reaches the place where he can trust no one. Himself a falsifier, he has no confidence in the word of others."—*The Acts of the Apostles*, p. 76.

The athlete.

The Greek word for "strive for masteries" is *athleō*, used only once (2 Timothy 2:5) in the New Testament, and giving us the English word *athlete*. Some people are naturally athletic and excel in physical gymnastics and sports, but even they must exercise to keep in good condition. Athletes who are champions in summer sports often put on excess weight in winter, and this overburden must be removed if they are to continue to excel. Likewise, those who are experts at winter sports cannot continue their prowess if they idle away the summer with overeating and lack of exercise.

The Christian life is somewhat similar; it is not, or it should not be, a matter of fits and starts, a period of godliness followed by a slack period of worldliness. Paul likened his experience to that of an athlete when he wrote to the Corinthians. After presenting the simile of a race, he continued, "I keep under my body, and bring it into subjection." 1 Corinthians 9:27. Paul had his eyes on the crown of eternal life to be awarded at the end of the heavenly race. As Dr. John Monsell, rector of St. Nicholas Church, Guildford, wrote in his hymn:

Run the straight race, through God's good grace,
Lift up thine eyes, and seek His face;
Life with its way before thee lies,
Christ is the path, and Christ the prize.
—*The New Advent Hymnal*, no. 511

The Christian race is more like a marathon than a sprint, for human life expectancy is comparatively long. Marathon runners do not suddenly decide to enter a contest. Just to finish the course, aside from winning, requires arduous training over months. Those foolhardy contestants who do not prepare, fall out or faint and never reach the finish line.

It is not surprising, therefore, that when we read in Hebrews 12:1 about running "the race that is set before us" we should be encouraged to do so "with patience." A sudden sprint may put us ahead of our fellow competitors, but there is a long, long course ahead, and we need to remind ourselves that Jesus, our Example, "endured." Verse 2. Throughout His earthly life, He manifested infinite patience.

In writing to Timothy, Paul especially emphasizes the quality of fairness without cheating. No man can enter the gates of Paradise on his own terms; he must comply with the conditions laid down in the Scriptures. "Of all the games instituted among the Greeks and the Romans, the foot-races were the most ancient and the most highly esteemed. . . . The contests were governed by strict regulations, from which there was no appeal. Those who desired their names entered as competitors for the prize, had first to undergo a severe preparatory training. Harmful indulgence of appetite, or any other gratification that would lower mental or physical vigor, was strictly forbidden. . . . The judges were seated near the goal, that they might watch the race from its beginning to its close, and give the prize to the true victor. If a man reached the goal first by taking an unlawful advantage, he was not awarded the prize."—*The Acts of the Apostles*, pp. 309, 310. So today tests are made even after a race to see whether horse or man has taken stimulating drugs. To be first past the winning post loses all significance if rules have been broken. Not only is the prize withheld, but the cheater's name becomes ignominious. The Christian, as an athlete running the Christian race, keeps himself pure, honest, patient, being strengthened by the One who has run the race before him.

The farmer.
While the simile of a farmer is used here (2 Timothy 2:6), the context shows that Paul is really saying two things: (a) that for Timothy to receive tithes and offerings for his support would not be dishonest or unlawful, and (b) that he must first practice what he preaches. He is a Christian soldier, living a life, not of luxury but of hardship, doing only those things that please his Master, dissociating himself from other interests that would bring him income and reward. Therefore, he has a perfect right to partake of such reward and sustenance as come from the faithful believers.

Paul had outlined the same principle in 1 Corinthians 9:7-11, where among other things he quoted from Deuteronomy 25:4: "Thou shalt not muzzle the ox when he treadeth out the corn." To this Paul added: "Doth God take care for oxen? Or saith he it altogether for our sakes? For our sakes, no doubt, this is written: that he that ploweth should plow in hope; and that he that thresheth in hope should be partaker of his hope." 1 Corinthians 9:9, 10. Even though on that particular occasion Paul did not take what was his just due, he made it clear that it was not only not wrong, but rather perfectly justifiable for the minister to reap the reward of his labor.

Timothy's spiritual ministry, sowing gospel seed, would naturally produce a harvest; and if part of this harvest were physical or "carnal things" (1 Corinthians 9:11), this would be simply the outworking of the law of nature, which is the law of God. "The farmer's produce feeds both himself and the rest of the world. If the farmer did not share in his produce, he would die and the rest of the world would go hungry."—*SDA Bible Commentary*, vol. 7, p. 334. Timothy was to partake of the physical food offered by his converts and continue to share the spiritual diet of which he was the minister.

It will likewise be obvious that the true minister will practice the truths which he preaches; otherwise, he cannot share his spiritual food with others. Not only does he himself suffer, but his listeners are spiritually starved also. The minister is unfair to himself and to his flock. His striving, his running, will be in vain. He will be exposed as a hypocrite.

The simile of the farmer also suggests patience, although this virtue is not mentioned here in the epistle. James mentioned it: "Behold, the husbandman waiteth for the precious fruit of the earth, and hath long patience for it." James 5:7. In his work he may not see the immediate result of his labors, but this should emphasize the virtue of cooperation instead of competition. Paul wrote to the Corinthian believers who were arguing among themselves about the preacher who had converted them, and thus dividing the church into factions. Paul suggested a sublime solution to the dispute: "I have planted, Apollos watered; but God gave the increase." 1 Corinthians 3:6. So patience is necessary, with trust in the Lord; the increase will come in His good time.

Our responsibility is to cultivate the soil of the heart, to sow the seed, and to water, then with patience and prayer to wait for the Lord to ripen the fruit. The wise man evidently met many farmers who were good at finding excuses for not sowing or reaping, for he observed: "He that observeth the wind shall not sow; and he that regardeth the clouds shall not reap." Ecclesiastes 11:4. Then follows his wise counsel: "In the morning sow thy seed, and in the evening withhold not thine hand: for thou knowest not whether shall prosper, either this or that, or whether they both shall be alike good." Verse 6. Isaiah speaks of the blessedness of those who sow beside all waters, trusting in the Creator to send His rain and snow from heaven to water and ripen the crops. See Isaiah 32:20. This is an object lesson of how He will cause the living Word of God to prosper, and not return unto Him void. See Isaiah 55:10, 11.

The Word of God

Uncertainty is a great destroyer of enthusiasm. Sure of his instructions, one may launch out eagerly to accomplish an assignment. But if doubts creep in, the worker hesitates; and if the doubts are not removed, he may abandon the job, unfinished.

No such doubts weaken Paul in the Roman dungeon. Confident of the Voice on the Damascus road, he set out years before to take the gospel to the Gentiles. Now in prison, held back on every side, his enemies determined to discourage him from preaching to anyone, he still presses forward with undiminished enthusiasm, as sure of God's word here as he has been anywhere.

Inspiration.

The Bible is different from any other book, for it is inspired by God. Using human instruments, He wrote His will in language we can understand. We often say that great poets, writers, and musicians are inspired; but this uses the word in a different sense. The human spirit and the talents God gives certain individuals may indeed rise to great heights; but God's Word transcends this kind of inspiration. God fills a prophet's mind with ideas or gives him a vision or a dream or sometimes sends a heavenly messenger to speak to him in human language, and the prophet uses his own words to express what he has learned. So the Bible is unique. It is God's principal way of communicating with mankind.

He uses other ways. One is nature, but this is distorted because of the entry of sin. Another is perfect, the incarnation of the Godhead in the person of Jesus of Nazareth. His earthly life demonstrated the perfect character of God and enabled mankind to understand the Father. Jesus said, "He that hath seen me hath seen the Father." John 14:9. However, this revelation occupied only a short 33 years in a small country, and we must depend on the Written Word to tell us more about God and His purpose for mankind.

A book that does this is certainly one above all others, for it contains solutions to the fundamental problems of life, death, destiny, eternity, sin, and salvation. It is more than a book of history, psychology, philosophy, or metaphysics. It is all these and more. It meets the need of king and commoner, of literate and illiterate, of saint and sinner, of Jew and Gentile, of man and woman, of old man and child. It is unique.

John Gibson Lockhart (1794-1854), who married Sir Walter Scott's daughter, wrote in his biography of his father-in-law about an incident that happened a few months before Scott's death. "He expressed a wish that I should read to him, and when I asked from what book, he said, 'Need you ask? There is but one.' I chose the 14th chapter of St. John's Gospel: he listened with mild devotion, and said when I had done—'Well, this is a great comfort.' "—*The Life of Sir Walter Scott*, p. 635. He who had written many thousands of words for the entertainment and enrichment of his fellow-countrymen recognized as he approached the valley of the shadow that he needed God's inspired words to comfort him.

Unity.
The remarkable unity of the Bible is even more astonishing when one realizes the different types of men who contributed to it and the length of time over which its portions were written. "The authorship of this book is wonderful. Here are words written by kings, by emperors, by princes, by poets, by sages, by philosophers, by fishermen, by statesmen; by men learned in the wisdom of Egypt, educated in the schools of Babylon, trained up at the feet of rabbis in Jerusalem. It was written by men in exile, in the desert, in shepherd's tents, in 'green pastures' and beside 'still waters.' Among its authors we find the tax-gatherer, the herdsman, the gatherer of sycamore fruit; we find poor men, rich men, statesmen, preachers, exiles, captains, legislators, judges; men of every grade and class are represented in this wonderful volume,

which is in reality a *library*, filled with history, genealogy, ethnology, law, ethics, prophecy, poetry, eloquence, medicine, sanitary science, political economy, and perfect rules for the conduct of personal and social life. It contains all kinds of writing; but what a jumble it would be if sixty-six books were written in this way by ordinary men!"—H. L. Hastings, *Will the Old Book Stand?* p. 21. "Here is a book coming from all quarters, written by men of all classes, scattered through a period of fifteen hundred years; and yet this book is fitted together as a wondrous and harmonious whole. . . . One mind inspired the whole book, one voice speaks in it all, and it is the voice of God speaking with resurrection power."—*Ibid.*, p. 22.

Dr. H. Grattan Guinness also emphasized the Bible's unity from a diversity of contributors: "The Bible is characterized by the unity of its theme. It unfolds a series of acts, all contributing to one design or end. This is the more remarkable on account of the variety in its authorship. Had the Bible been written in one age, or by one person, its unity might not so much surprise us. But the Bible is a collection of books which were written by different persons, in different languages, in different lands, and at different times. Seventeen centuries were employed in its composition. The subjects it embraces are so numerous as to give it a cyclopaedic character. Yet from first to last that marvellous collection of books is occupied with one subject, animated by one Spirit, directed to one object or end."—*Creation Centred in Christ*, p. 84.

Sound words of truth.

Sound or healthy words have an uplifting effect, and the words of the Scriptures are to the spirit what the heavenly manna was to the Israelites, a necessary daily food. Job said: "I have esteemed the words of his mouth more than my necessary food." Job 23:12. The newborn Christian, like the newborn babe, is sustained on milk, an illustration used by Peter when he encouraged the believers that "as newborn babes" they should "desire the sincere milk of the word, that ye may grow thereby." 1 Peter 2:2.

But a stronger diet is required by the more mature Christian who has imbibed the first principles of Christian growth. "For every one that useth milk is unskillful in the word of righteousness: for he is a babe. But strong meat belongeth to them that are of full age, even those who by reason of use have their senses exercised to discern both good and evil." Hebrews 5:13, 14. Paul here is reproaching his hearers for not advancing in the Christian way to the point where they could be teachers of others, ministering the Word of God to those who are babes in Christ. See verse 12.

That hearing the Word of God creates an appetite for more is illustrated in the story of Mary Jones. This young Welsh girl wanted a copy of the Word of God so badly that she walked more than twenty miles from her home to the minister's in order to purchase a copy. The Reverend Thomas Charles (1755-1833), a Methodist minister of Bala in north Wales, asked another young girl if she could tell him the text he had preached on the previous Sunday. He was amazed to learn that because the weather had been bad she had been unable to follow her practice of walking seven miles to a friend's home once a week to read a Welsh Bible. These and other incidents led to the formation of the British and Foreign Bible Society and its plan to place a copy of the Scriptures without note or comment in the hands of everyone who wanted one in his own tongue at a price he could afford. So blessed has been this project that Scripture portions are now available in 1600 languages and dialects, and millions of copies are distributed every year.

Care must be taken in "rightly dividing the word of truth." 2 Timothy 2:15. It is not difficult to make the Bible mean something it does not mean, by placing unrelated parts together or out of context or reading only part of a verse or sentence or spiritualizing away the meaning of a passage. Shakespeare in his play *The Merchant of Venice* has Shylock the Jew cite the story of Jacob, who placed peeled branches of various trees in the watering troughs in the belief that the cattle, sheep, and goats would give birth to speckled offspring. See Genesis 30:37-39; but see also chapter 31:10-12 for the true explanation. Shylock used this story to justify his practice of usury; he said he was simply making his money breed and multiply as fast as Jacob's ewes. Antonio's answer was very appropriate, not only for Shylock, but also for those who do not rightly divide the Word of truth:

The devil can cite scripture for his purpose.
An evil soul producing holy witness
Is like a villain with a smiling cheek—
A goodly apple rotten at the heart:
O, what a goodly outside falsehood hath!
—*Act I, scene 3, lines 100-105.*

The fact that the Bible is sometimes used for such purposes—
that is, to give an implication of truth—shows in what respect the
Scriptures are held. The mere quotation of them suggests truth,
even though it may be mishandled. How much greater good can
come when these inspired words are rightly divided, given their
real meaning, and used for their intended purpose.

Saving truth.

Paul complimented Timothy on having known the Scriptures
since he was a child (see 2 Timothy 3:15), for they had made him
wise. But note this was not wisdom in the sense of having profound knowledge, nor even of possessing discreet judgment;
Timothy was "wise unto salvation" through faith. For "faith
cometh by hearing, and hearing by the word of God." Romans
10:17. The purpose of the Word is to save the reader, to point out
to him the road that leads to the heavenly home, the means by
which he can escape the curse of sin and the wiles of the devil.
Furthermore, the Word explains itself so that no one can plead
that he is not a learned theologian or expositor and therefore cannot find the way of salvation. While admittedly some parts are
difficult to understand, yet by comparing one scripture with other
scriptures the meaning can be unraveled.

Jesus gave us the key in His own use of the Old Testament. To
the discouraged disciples on their way to Emmaus He "expounded unto them in all the scriptures the things concerning himself." Luke 24:27. He used the words written by Moses and the
prophets and showed how they foretold with great exactitude the
events of the sufferings and resurrection of the Messiah. Earlier
He had bidden His disciples to search the Scriptures so that they
might be ready to face future trouble. Referring to Daniel the
prophet, our Lord had said: "Whoso readeth, let him understand." Matthew 24:15.

The effect of saving truth is well shown in the experience of the great evangelist and hymn-writer Charles Wesley. On the day of his conversion in May 1738, he wrote these lines:

> No condemnation now I dread;
> Jesus, and all in Him, is mine!
> Alive in Him, my living Head,
> And clothed in righteousness divine,
> Bold I approach th'eternal throne,
> And claim the crown through Christ my own.
> —*The New Advent Hymnal*, no. 698

His joyful spirit arose again a year later on the first anniversary of this conversion experience:

> On this glad day the glorious Sun
> Of righteousness arose;
> On my benighted soul He shone
> And filled it with repose.
>
> O for a thousand tongues to sing
> My great Redeemer's praise.
> —*Singing With Understanding,* p. 120 and
> *The Church Hymnal,* no. 155

The profitable Word.

The Codex Sinaiticus is a copy of the Bible written by hand sometime around the year 325. Forty-three leaves were obtained by the German textual critic Tischendorf in 1844 in the monastery of St. Catherine at the foot of Mount Sinai. Some of the sheets were moldy with age and about to be burned. Tischendorf obtained the rest of the manuscript in 1859 and took it to Germany to be copied. By arrangement with the head of the monastery, the valuable manuscript was donated to the imperial library at St. Petersburg (now Leningrad). It is one of the oldest parchment copies of the Bible in existence and proved very profitable to the government of the Soviet Republic. They sold it to the British government in 1933 for £100,000. Placed on exhibition in the British Museum, it attracted long queues of persons eager to see such an old text of the famous Book, even though most who looked at its beautiful Greek letters were unable to read them.

The Word of God is profitable in another sense than that measured by money. But this value comes only to those who read it.

With so many translations and paraphrases extant today, most of them true to the original, there is little excuse for Westerners to be ignorant of the Bible.

But what advantage does a man have who does not read the Bible over the man who cannot read it? We talk glibly of the ignorant savage and deplore his ignorance of the Scriptures. Unfortunately too many good, moral Christians are equally ignorant of the profit that the Word of God could bring them.

Its profit has to do, of course, with the spiritual life, with its teaching about the nature of God, His promises to sinners, the gift of His Son for our redemption, and the way of escape from certain death. Its profit lies also in the reproof it gives, even though this may shock us, as Nathan's words shocked David when he revealed the sin that the king thought he had concealed. His words, "Thou art the man" (2 Samuel 12:7), pierce our own hearts when we read of the standard God has set for His people and consider the feeble efforts we make to repel the enemy. It is said that the American humorist Mark Twain was surprised that so many critics of the Bible were worried by the difficult Scripture passages they could not understand. As for him, he said, it was the things in the Bible that he did understand that worried him. Apparently he felt condemned by the clear statements about sin and sinners.

The Word of God is not negative only; it points to the correct way of life. It gives the perfect example of the Lord Jesus living in human flesh, tempted by the devil, subject to all kinds of affliction, but keeping faith in His heavenly Father, an example "that ye should follow his steps." 1 Peter 2:21. It gives us many examples of men and women who, though faulty, were nevertheless accounted righteous because they trusted in Christ's forgiveness and His power to save.

Even the noble patriarchs and the heroes of faith have their sins pointed out. They are shown to be vulnerable to Satan's deceptions. They fall into sin. But they are victors in the end, and their faith is accounted unto them for righteousness.

Well would it be for each of us to ask himself the meaning of the word *profit*. In the light of the Lord's question: "What is a man profited, if he shall gain the whole world, and lose his own soul?" (Matthew 16:26), we see that profit is to be measured in terms of eternity, not in terms of gold or silver or power or authority in this world. The Bible is profitable in the best and highest and most enduring meaning of the word.

The unbound Book.

Living in the age of printing and instant photocopying, we are inclined to forget the tiresome labor that was necessary to produce a copy of a written work in olden times. Even though there were so many illiterates who could not read the copies anyway, there was also a nucleus of scholars who copied manuscripts for the benefit of their contemporaries and of posterity. What a blessing—and to some extent, a curse—came upon the world in the 1450s when Johann Gutenberg invented the art of printing from movable type. The Bible in Latin was one of the first works to come off his printing press and is now among the world's most valuable rare books.

John Wycliffe (1325-84), who translated the Bible from the Latin Vulgate into English, was much handicapped by the time required to make copies. "At last the work was completed—the first English translation of the Bible ever made. The word of God was opened to England. The Reformer [Wycliffe] . . . had placed in the hands of the English people a light which should never be extinguished. In giving the Bible to his countrymen, he had done more to break the fetters of ignorance and vice, more to liberate and elevate his country, than was ever achieved by the most brilliant victories in fields of battle."—*The Great Controversy*, p. 88.

About a century and a half later, William Tyndale (1492-1536) translated most of the Scriptures from the original Hebrew and Greek and was able to disseminate the Word much more rapidly because of the invention of printing. Even though copies were bought up so they could be burned, the income from the sale enabled further printing to continue. In the providence of God His Word is not bound. It is the vehicle that makes known His will, and it has withstood attacks from all quarters to become the world's best-selling book.

"The bishop of Durham at one time bought of a bookseller who was a friend of Tyndale his whole stock of Bibles, for the purpose of destroying them, supposing that this would greatly hinder the work. But, on the contrary, the money thus furnished, purchased material for a new and better edition, which, but for this, could not have been published. When Tyndale was afterward made a prisoner, his liberty was offered him on condition that he would reveal the names of those who had helped him meet the expense of printing his Bibles. He replied that the bishop of Durham had done more than any other person; for by paying a large price for the books left on hand, he had enabled him to go on with good courage."—*The Great Controversy*, p. 247.

Through the providence of God, His Word has been disseminated by faithful witnesses even at the risk of their lives. The human instruments may be persecuted and killed, but the Written Word continues, speaking its message for all who will hear. It is God's plan that the "gospel of the kingdom shall be preached in all the world" before the end of time. Matthew 24:14. "People everywhere are to have the Bible opened to them. . . . The truth comprised in the first, second, and third angels' messages must go to every nation, kindred, tongue, and people; it must lighten the darkness of every continent and extend to the islands of the sea. Nothing of human invention must be allowed to retard the work."—*Testimonies for the Church*, vol. 6, pp. 133, 134.

Because God's Word is unbound, it stretches the minds that grapple with its truths. "Youthful minds fail to reach their noblest development when they neglect the highest source of wisdom,— the word of God. That we are in God's world, in the presence of the Creator; that we are made in His likeness; that He watches over us and loves us and cares for us,—these are wonderful themes for thought, and lead the mind into broad, exalted fields of meditation. He who opens mind and heart to the contemplation of such themes as these will never be satisfied with trivial, sensational subjects."—*Counsels to Parents and Teachers*, p. 139.

Human Philosophy

Something like ten years passed between Paul's interrupted journey to Damascus intent on destroying Christians, and his first missionary journey to Europe establishing Christian churches. He spent three of those years in Arabia and close to seven back in Tarsus. Much of this isolated decade was devoted to studying the Old Testament, searching for the truth about God.

The vast fund of sanctified information Paul acquired at that time proved of enormous value later as he met minds saturated with the philosophies of the world; and it brought sustaining peace and trust in the dungeon's dark and final days.

The search for truth.

Man is endowed with a spirit of inquiry. When Moses as a shepherd saw a bush burning in the hot desert it was nothing out of the ordinary, but the fact that it was not consumed (see Exodus 2:2) *was* unusual, and his attention was arrested. Here was a phenomenon he had not encountered before "in all the wisdom of the Egyptians." Acts 7:22. "Moses saw a bush in flames, branches, foliage, and trunk, all burning, yet seeming not to be consumed."—*Patriarchs and Prophets*, p. 251.

This extraordinary sight would have attracted anyone's attention. But the whole world of nature is full of phenomena, common and uncommon. Mankind's urge to discover has led to wonderful advances in science, where theories can be tested; and to an increase in knowledge in other disciplines, where it is more difficult to put theories to the test.

This insatiable curiosity has led to speculation which is not always restrained by facts, and the history of the search for knowledge is strewn with discarded theories once held to be absolute truth. This is even true of books about the Bible. The shelves of libraries are loaded with commentaries expounding different authors' ideas on what inspired writers wrote, or what they intended to write! As the wise man said: "Of making many books there is no end." Ecclesiastes 12:12. His comments in the preceding verses describe his care to select material so that in his books would be found only "acceptable words . . . : upright, even words of truth . . . words of the wise." Verses 10, 11. We must always remember that the words of man are liable to error, "but the word of our God shall stand for ever." Isaiah 40:8.

In an age when every wind of doctrine is blowing and unsettling the faith of some, it is well to remember that there are certain landmarks of our faith that are not open to question. They are not negotiable; they are incontrovertible.

Profane words. 2 Timothy 2:16.

The original word for *profane* means to step on the threshold, in the sense that anyone can enter the building and is not barred. Hence it has the sense of common as opposed to limited access, especially in respect to religious sites. The English word literally means "outside the temple." It refers to activities that are not suitable for a place of worship. Such secular works or words are not necessarily blasphemous, although that meaning has become attached also to the word *profanity*.

In the context in which *profane* is used in Paul's final letter to Timothy (see 2 Timothy 2:16), it means that which is godless, outside the realm of religious discussion. A minister of God should be engaged in things of the church and not be sidetracked by worldly philosophies that are human and not divine. Furthermore, because they are human, they will be as diverse as humans are and will lead to diverse conclusions. While philosophers' reasonings may be based on observable facts, they are limited, because other facts are yet to be found.

In addition, human beings, no matter how objective they try to be, are guided by their feelings and prejudices, and one can derive an optimistic, whereas another may produce a pessimistic result, all from the same observations. This is particularly the case when the thinker deals with the past or future. See, for example, the contradictory theories of the origin of the earth and the solar system, conclusions which cannot be tested and are vain speculation with only a small degree of plausibility. The vain babblings, or sound without meaning, are reminiscent of Shakespeare's statement that life "is a tale told by an idiot, full of sound and fury, signifying nothing,"—*Macbeth*, act V, scene v, 1. 17.

Paul was accused of using vain babblings in Athens, although the word *babbler* (Acts 17:18) used in the King James Version is translated from a different Greek word from that used in 2 Timothy 2:16. The reference to Paul means "speaker of seeds," that is, a person who talks of small, trifling matters, as a bird picks here and there for seeds. To some of his hearers, it was indeed idle chatter and foolishness, but "the foolishness of God is wiser than men." 1 Corinthians 1:25. Paul's "babbling" led to godliness, whereas the unbeliever's "profane and vain babblings" lead to even more ungodliness or profanity.

Harmful nonessentials.

Arguing about profane topics is not only "to no profit" but may result in actual harm, especially to the one who promotes a peculiar interpretation of Scripture. To say, for example, that the two pence given by the Samaritan to the innkeeper (see Luke 10:35) represent the two sacraments given by Jesus to the Christian church, is pure fiction. Or to find some significance in the fact that 153 great fish were netted by the disciples after the resurrection (see John 21:11) is to bring reproach upon biblical exegesis. Foolish questions are an attempt by the enemy to sidetrack the witness for truth, and should be recognized as such. Avoiding them is not a form of cowardice, but a strong form of courage.

"Some who in Paul's day listened to the truth, raised questions of no vital importance, presenting the ideas and opinions of men, and seeking to divert the mind of the teacher from the great truths of the gospel, to the discussion of nonessential theories and the settlement of unimportant disputes. Paul knew that the laborer for God must be wise enough to see the design of the enemy, and refuse to be misled or diverted. The conversion of souls must be the burden of his work; he must preach the word of God, but avoid controversy."—*Gospel Workers*, pp. 311, 312.

Adam Clarke wrote: "It is very remarkable how often and with what seriousness, the apostle cautions Timothy against disputes in religion, which surely was not without some such design as this, to show us that religion consists more in believing and practising what God requires than in subtle disputes."—*The Holy Bible, Commentary and Critical Notes, the New Testament*, vol. III, p. 480.

Distortions of truth.

False interpretations, given with a pious assurance that they are the will of God, are highly dangerous. Slowly but surely they lead to destruction. Sometimes the process is accelerated, as in the dreadful example of the Jones cult. Persuaded by a fallible human being, Jones's misled followers committed mass suicide under the impression that they were entering a new and perfect world.

Religious experience which depends solely on the word of another or on a corrupt and false explanation of God's Word is a badly corroding experience. Corroding and rusting are slow, insidious processes of destruction. They often go unnoticed, or, if noticed, are ignored for the time being. Attention can be given at some more convenient season. But these insidious forces often terminate with a surprising effect. A tree in the forest suddenly topples. Why did it die so quickly? Examination shows it to be rotten at the roots. This was no sudden death. Although seconds before it collapsed it appeared to be as healthy as its upright neighbors, it had been ill for a long time. Snow may cover a deep crevasse. Thinking it perfectly safe, the unwary traveler steps onto it and disappears into the frozen depths below. Again, the process is as the poet Henry Wadsworth Longfellow says, in a more cheerful context dealing with success rather than failure:

> The heights by great men reached and kept
> Were not attained by sudden flight,
> But they, while their companions slept,
> Were toiling upward in the night.
> —*The Ladder of St. Augustine*

The dreadful depths, likewise, are not reached suddenly. Beware the cankerous, gangrenous teachings of man! They slowly but surely eat away faith in God's Word.

Gossip and rumor are destroyers also, and words that easily escape our lips cannot be recalled. Often they are repeated and magnified out of all proportion and speeded on by others to perform a disastrous work.

> Good name in man or woman, dear my lord,
> Is the immediate jewel in their souls:
> Who steals my purse steals trash; 'tis something, nothing,
> 'Twas mine, 'tis his, and has been slave to thousands,
> But he that filches from me my good name
> Robs me of that which not enriches him,
> And makes me poor indeed.
> —*Othello*, act II, scene iii, ll. 153-159.

Majors and minors. 2 Timothy 2:23.

When foolish questions posed for the sake of argument are compared with honest, sincere questions asked to arrive at truth, it is easy to see how time-wasting and unprofitable the former are. While they may provoke discussion, their contribution is usually negligible.

When Jesus rebuked the scribes and Pharisees, one of the points He criticized was their concentration on matters of minor importance. While it is necessary to attend to these details, they must never crowd out the major, essential factors of religious life. "Woe unto you, scribes and Pharisees, hypocrites! for ye pay tithe of mint and anise and cummin, and have omitted the weightier matters of the law, judgment, mercy, and faith: these ought ye to have done, and not to leave the other undone." Matthew 23:23. They had substituted the minor for the major, then offered those small aspects of religion as serving for the whole duty of man.

Just how foolish were their actions is shown by the hyperbole Jesus used when He said they were so meticulous as to strain their drinking water to exclude a small gnat—a quite laudable action—but swallowed without protest a much larger and more undesirable source of pollution, a camel! See verse 24.

"The Pharisees . . . went to unwarranted extremes. Among other things the people were required to strain all the water used, lest it should contain the smallest insect, which might be classed with the unclean animals."—*The Desire of Ages*, p. 617.

"Without foundation men will make statements with all the positiveness of truth; but it is of no use to argue with them concerning their spurious assertions. The best way to deal with error is to present the truth, and leave wild ideas to die out for want of notice. . . . The more the erroneous assertions of opposers, and of those who rise up among us to deceive souls, are repeated, the better the cause of error is served."—*Testimonies to Ministers*, p. 165.

"Angels of God are watching you, and they understand how to impress those whose opposition you refuse to meet with arguments. Dwell not on the negative points of questions that arise, but gather to your minds affirmative truths. . . . We strengthen their arguments when we repeat what they say. It may be that the very man who is opposing you will carry your words home, and be converted to the sensible truth that has reached his understanding."—*Gospel Workers*, p. 358.

Unspoken questions.

While we may be aware of foolish questions people ask us to embarrass us or to start an argument, we must also be on guard lest we ask ourselves foolish questions. In times of personal perplexity, we may be inclined to question whether we have followed cunningly devised fables. We may begin to wonder whether what we have held as truth is really unassailable. We may compare our lot in life with that of ungodly persons who seem to be prospering much more than we are.

David found himself in this plight but did not remain there. He found his way out. Then he looked at himself and admitted: "So foolish was I, and ignorant; I was as a beast before thee." Psalm 73:22. The earlier verses of this psalm reveal the cause of his discouragement. His steps had almost slipped. But when he "went into the sanctuary of God" (verse 17) and caught a glimpse of the end of the wicked, he saw that they surely were in slippery places (see verse 18). His foolish thoughts, or lack of thought—for he likened himself to a thoughtless animal—were resolved by looking at God's positive attitude and action.

The Bible is a collection of books, and it is well that we scrutinize it carefully, just as we do other documents of great age. We should analyze it, compare it with itself, place each section in its historical, geographical, and social setting, and exercise our God-given powers of intellect as we study it. But—and this is a most important reservation—we must realize that the Bible is a unique book, preserved miraculously, penned by different writers who wrote as they were moved by the Holy Ghost. It was given by God for a purpose that supersedes all academic approaches to its study. If the Written Word of God does not reveal to us the incarnate Word of God, our study is merely a theoretical exercise of no spiritual value.

This, indeed, was the charge leveled against the scribes by our Lord when He said that they searched the Scriptures to obtain eternal life but failed to find there the One who alone could give eternal life. See John 5:39.

This thought was well expressed by Dr. A. T. Pierson: "There never was or will be another book that combines the human and divine elements as this Book does. When therefore we are told that it must be studied just as other books are, that is exactly what we deny. It must be studied as no other book is, because it constitutes a class by itself, and can be classed with no others."—*The Bible and Spiritual Criticism*, p. 14.

The bias of preconceived notions.

It is possible to be so absorbed in Bible study that we place our own interpretations on what we read, not verifying them by comparison with other scriptures, but being biased by our own preconceived notions. "Especially should we entreat the Lord for wisdom to understand His word. Here are revealed the wiles of the tempter and the means by which he may be successfully resisted. Satan is an expert in quoting scripture, placing his own interpretation upon passages, by which he hopes to cause us to stumble."—*The Great Controversy*, p. 530. He had blinded the scribes so that they revered the word but reviled the Word.

Another very common misuse of the Bible is not to use it, but to keep it as a kind of talisman, a book on which to swear to tell the truth, a kind of magic protection. It has often been said that he who does not read has no advantage over him who cannot. We love to support the Bible societies of our different countries for their worthy aim to place a copy of the Scriptures, or at least a portion, in the hand of every person on earth. With what joy these copies are received by those formerly ignorant of salvation. For many, this is the Book from which they learn to read. "Can we, whose souls are lighted with wisdom from on high" (*The Advent Hymnal*, no. 285) deny ourselves the "lamp of life" by just possessing the volume in our homes, but neglecting to read it? Is not this placing ourselves in a position as benighted as those who have never had access to the Word of life?

We deplore the action of religious organizations that forbid their lay members to read the Bible on the ground that it is a book capable of understanding only by trained priests or learned theologians. We stand aghast that Bibles were publicly burned in the days of William Tyndale lest the laity obtain copies. Are we not doing the same disfavor to ourselves when we keep the Book of books untouched, gathering dust, its pages never opened? Surely this is one of the gravest misuses of the treasure that God has so graciously given us.

To offer the excuse that there are things in the Bible that we cannot explain and that we do not wish to undermine our own faith by examining them is placing ourselves on dangerous ground. "While God has given ample evidence for faith, He will never remove all excuse for unbelief. All who look for hooks to hang their doubts upon will find them. And those who refuse to accept and obey God's word until every objection has been removed, and there is no longer an opportunity for doubt, will never come to the light. . . . Instead of questioning and caviling concerning that which they do not understand, let them give heed to the light which already shines upon them, and they will receive greater light."—*The Great Controversy*, pp. 527, 528.

Human philosophy lacks the divine touch of certainty, whereas God's Word and its divine philosophy guide the simple wayfaring man unerringly on the road to Zion. See Isaiah 35:8.

Vessels of Honor

We tend to glorify Paul for all the wonderful work he accomplished, all the people he converted, all the churches he founded, all the books of the Bible he wrote. He suffered so many trials in the course of these good deeds—so many shipwrecks, beatings, stonings, and imprisonments—that he might have been justified had he hugged to himself whatever small praise he received. But that wasn't his way. Every letter he wrote credits fellow workers for assisting him. His last, the second to Timothy, is no exception. Perhaps the memory of these faithful workers brightened his cell and cheered his final days.

Faithful helpers. 2 Timothy 2:20.
Paul reminded Timothy, as he had the church in Corinth when it was beset by controversy, that the members of the Christian church are different one from another. This difference should not lead to dissension, as it did in Corinth, but to a harmony of complementary functions. Paul listed several gifts in Ephesians 4:8-11. He added to the list in 1 Corinthians 12:28. Here, in addition to the obviously important gifts, he mentioned one which is often forgotten, namely "helps."

The word is derived from a verb that means "to take hold of," or "to share." In 1 Timothy 6:2 it is translated "partaker." A help therefore is one who shares the burden of another, who takes hold of his load and helps to carry it.

This function in the church may pass unnoticed by many, for it does not involve appearance in public or preaching to large congregations. However, in the Lord's sight it marks a vessel of honor. Did even the great apostle himself overlook "helps" in the questions he asked in 1 Corinthians 12:29, 30? He repeated most of the other spiritual gifts but left out "helps." Certainly, whatever the gift, each member should be a helper and a burdenbearer.

During World War I many soldiers of no special rank lost their lives in the awful carnage. In order to recognize their sacrifice, the body of one nameless soldier was buried among the kings in Westminster Abbey, in the most sacred of England's tombs, named the tomb of the Unknown Soldier. Other countries followed this practice, each giving honor to an unknown soldier whose last resting place is now with the great and mighty of their land. He is nameless, but he played a significant and honorable part in the service of his country.

Very little is recorded about most of the people mentioned in 2 Timothy 4. They probably did not accomplish a dramatic work, such as building a huge ark on land with no human possibility of launching it; or renouncing the throne of a mighty empire and returning forty years later to lead a nation out of slavery; or calling fire down from heaven to consume a water-sodden sacrifice. They were ordinary men and women, undistinguished among the multitude of their peers, like so many of us. But they were loyal and faithful, good sheaves for the Master's harvest, worthy trophies gained by the apostle Paul. They were conscientiously imitating his manner of life. They were among those to whom the Lord will say in the final day of reckoning: "Well done, good and faithful servant." Matthew 25:23.

"Paul carried with him the atmosphere of heaven. All who associated with him felt the influence of his union with Christ. The fact that his own life exemplified the truth he proclaimed, gave convincing power to his preaching. Here lies the power of the truth. The unstudied, unconscious influence of a holy life is the most convincing sermon that can be given in favor of Christianity. Argument, even when unanswerable, may provoke only opposition; but a godly example has a power that it is impossible wholly to resist."—*Gospel Workers*, p. 59.

Christians following this superb example are not concerned with praise or credit for work accomplished. If credit should mistakenly rest on another's shoulders, what matter? The important thing is that the work has been done. Their commendation is written in the Scriptures in parentheses, as if it were an interruption in the flow of thought. It is found in Hebrews 11:38: "Of whom the world was not worthy." Such will certainly enter into the joy of their Lord.

The verb from which we obtain our word *help* is also used in Acts 20:35, where Paul, in his final, emotional address to the Ephesian elders, admonished them "to support" the weak. Any supporter of this nature is a vessel of honor which the Master can use in His service.

Onesiphorus. 2 Timothy 1:16-18. This friendly soul oozed hospitality and kindness. He even brought comfort to the apostle, who of all people was a great comforter of others. "The desire for love and sympathy is implanted in the heart by God Himself. Christ, in His hour of agony in Gethsemane, longed for the sympathy of His disciples. And Paul, though apparently indifferent to hardship and suffering, yearned for sympathy and companionship. The visit of Onesiphorus, testifying to his fidelity at a time of loneliness and desertion, brought gladness and cheer to one who had spent his life in service for others."—*The Acts of the Apostles*, p. 491.

The conduct of Onesiphorus evidently was consistent, for his home was a place of welcome. Like Abraham, he was "not forgetful to entertain strangers." Hebrews 13:2. He was an excellent example of Peter's instruction: "Use hospitality one to another without grudging." 1 Peter 4:9. He was not kind in order to obtain a reward or to receive honor from the church, but simply because kindness was an outworking of his own helpful nature. To be kind brought him and his household pleasure, for he was "a lover of hospitality, a lover of good men." Titus 1:8.

Titus. 2 Timothy 4:10. Titus was a non-Jew whom Paul—with the support of the apostles in Jerusalem—had refused to be circumcised. Paul insisted, against great pressure from the Judaizers, that Titus be a living example that salvation is by faith in Jesus and not by works of the flesh. See Galatians 2:2-5. He gave Paul invaluable assistance. He built bridges to connect different modes of thought. He removed walls that divided church members. He remained strong when controversy raged about him. Paul's counsel evidently had had a good effect on this worthy helper: "Let no man despise thee." Titus 2:15.

Luke. 2 Timothy 4:11. Because he traveled with Paul, we know more of Luke than we might otherwise. Inspiration informs us that he did not volunteer to become a missionary: "The apostle Paul heard of his [Luke's] skill as a physician, and sought him out as one to whom the Lord had entrusted a special work. . . . In his work as a physician, he ministered to the sick, and then prayed for the healing power of God to rest upon the afflicted ones. . . . Luke's success as a physician gained for him many opportunities for preaching Christ among the heathen."—*The Ministry of Healing,* pp. 140, 141.

His professional skill, however, did not excuse him from hardships nor give him favored treatment. He accompanied Paul in whatever situation arose in the course of their endeavors. Tradition says that Luke was of Antioch, and Colossians 4:11, 14 seems to imply that he was a Gentile. What a blessing this educated doctor was to Paul in his last days on earth, when the devil made him the object of his supreme attack, knowing that he had but a short time in which to dishearten the apostle. "Only Luke is with me," Paul wrote. 2 Timothy 4:11. What a comfort this one man was!

Mark. 2 Timothy 4:11. With what promise this young man started his missionary career! In the company of his relative, Barnabas, he was assured of personal attention and help. Returning from Jerusalem with Barnabas and Paul (see Acts 12:25), then continuing with them on their successful mission to Cyprus, he went on to Asia Minor; but this was the end for him. While it is true that a journey over water does not make a missionary, this time it evidently unmade one. Later we read of violent storms in the Mediterranean (see Acts 27:14, 15, 18), but inspiration is silent on whether this sea trip was stormy. At all events, Mark's promising start came to a disastrous end. Committees today would write this young man off as a failure. Paul refused to take him on his second missionary journey, because he "went not with them to the work." Acts 15:38. But with further encouragement from Barnabas, Mark made another beginning on the same island where he had enjoyed initial success. Building on this, he finally received the marvelous accolade from the greatest missionary of them all: "Take Mark, and bring him with thee: for he is profitable to me for the ministry." 2 Timothy 4:11.

What an encouragement this experience is to all who are beset by discouragement and apparent failure, and looking inward, see no sense in trying again. If they would look upward, their spiritual vision would catch a brighter picture. "Into the experience of all there come times of keen disappointment and utter discouragement,—days when sorrow is the portion, and it is hard to believe that God is still the kind benefactor of His earthborn children; days when troubles harass the soul, till death seems preferable to life. It is then that many lose their hold on God, and are brought into the slavery of doubt, the bondage of unbelief. Could we at such times discern with spiritual insight the meaning of God's providences, we should see angels seeking to save us from ourselves, striving to plant our feet upon a foundation more firm than the everlasting hills."—*Prophets and Kings*, p. 162.

Elijah in his depression and utter discouragement was privileged to see a real angel; he took fresh heart and applied the "sure remedy,—faith, prayer, work. Faith and activity will impart assurance and satisfaction that will increase day by day."—*Ibid.*, p. 164. The trials that beset us are God's workmen to help us see ourselves as God sees us, to help us correct the defects in our characters, and to have the dross purged out. "The fact that we are called upon to endure trial shows that the Lord Jesus sees in us something precious, which He desires to develop. . . . He does not cast worthless stones into His furnace. It is valuable ore that He refines."—*The Ministry of Healing*, p. 471. This vessel, John Mark, could have degenerated into a vessel of dishonor, but because he tried again, he was formed into a vessel of honor.

Tychicus. 2 Timothy 4:12. This helper in the church was a good substitute. He could follow successful workers without disappointing the congregations who had lost a beloved leader. The work of the gospel does not suffer loss when ministers like him are moved from place to place. This takes talent, for there is always a temptation to criticize, or at least, not to speak well of one's predecessor, or to lay the blame for lack of progress on the poor foundation laid by the one who is no longer there.

It appears too that Tychicus was a very sympathetic person. He could feel the afflictions of others and knew what to say—or not to say—in times of distress. Many people are proud of speaking from the shoulder, and forthrightness is indeed praiseworthy; but Tychicus spoke from the heart and to the heart. His name means "fortunate," but it seems that his fellow-workers and those to whom he ministered were the fortunate ones, to have such an understanding brother as their friend. What better testimony could be borne than that he "stood nobly by the apostle."—*The Acts of the Apostles*, p. 455.

Aquila and Priscilla. 2 Timothy 4:19. The hands of this pair of loyal workers must have been roughened by their long toil at tentmaking. But their hands were tender in the sense that they were praying hands, outstretched to help others, not least Paul himself. Expelled from Rome by the decree of the Emperor Claudius (see Acts 18:2), they set up home in Corinth and continued their trade. They were never ministers, but they were tremendous help to the church, taking some of the ordinary burdens and leaving the ministers to proclaim the word of God. But they were not content merely to perform secular tasks. Having found Apollos at Ephesus and heard him preach, they realized that, mighty in the Scriptures though he was, he was ignorant of much of the way of God. Unafraid to share their faith, they "expounded unto him the way of God more perfectly." Acts 18:26. This fellow Jew, leaving them, crossed over to Greece and in his public lectures convinced the Jews, "shewing by the scriptures that Jesus was Christ." Verse 28. Through Aquila and Priscilla's teaching, Apollos "obtained a clearer understanding of the Scriptures, and became one of the ablest advocates of the Christian faith."—*The Acts of the Apostles*, p. 270.

Erastus. 2 Timothy 4:20. Not only does Paul rescue Erastus from anonymity, secular history has also preserved his name on a paving block in old Corinth. But how much more important it is to have our names written in the book of life! Paul mentions another fellowworker by name, Clement. See Philippians 4:3. Many other early Christians, including faithful women, are inscribed in the book of life, even though they find no place in Paul's epistle. "Rejoice," said our Lord to the seventy disciples, "because your names are written in heaven." Luke 10:20. How frail and ephemeral are names written on parchment or stone. Shelley, with fine irony, describes the transient nature of fame and power in his sonnet on "Ozymandias of Egypt":

> I met a traveler from an antique land
> Who said: Two vast and trunkless legs of stone
> Stand in the desert. Near them, on the sand,
> Half sunk, a shattered visage lies, whose frown
> And wrinkled lip and sneer of cold command
> Tell that its sculptor well those passions read
> Which yet survive, stamped on these lifeless things,
> The hand that mocked them and the heart that fed;
> And on the pedestal these words appear:
> "My name is Ozymandias, king of kings:
> Look on my works, ye Mighty, and despair!"
> Nothing beside remains. Round the decay
> Of that colossal wreck, boundless and bare,
> The lone and level sands stretch far away.

Vessels of dishonor.

The contrast between the two kinds of vessels seems to be the quality of permanence; gold and silver may become tarnished but can be cleaned, whereas wood and earth may become split or broken and must be thrown away. Paul indicates that vessels of dishonor may change to vessels of honor, and the converse is equally possible.

Demas illustrates one who did not "purge himself." 2 Timothy 2:21. He had been an associate of the apostle, but forsook him, his love for the world stronger than his love for the work of God. See 2 Timothy 4:10. We must watch lest being a golden vessel we imagine that we are important. We are still vessels, and our function is to contain. A flowerpot may be beautiful, but the flowers it displays are the center of attraction.

A similar illustration is a channel that conducts life-giving water. The channel is not necessarily beautiful, even though an aqueduct towering over the surrounding countryside is a magnificent sight. Its beauty and blessing lie in its function—to provide life. A long-time Christian, not notably talented but always faithful, described himself this way: "I am a very small vessel and cannot hold very much, but I can overflow a lot." This should be the Christian's prayer:

> Make me a channel of blessing, I pray,
> Make me a channel of blessing today,
> My life confessing,
> My service blessing,
> Make me a channel of blessing today.
> —H. G. Smith in *Alexander's Hymns No. 3*, no. 20

Perhaps we think we should be considered golden vessels rather than silver ones and should receive greater credit or more responsibility in the work of the Lord. We need not worry about such things, for such thoughts will lead to inefficiency. "If any are qualified for a higher position, the Lord will lay the burden, not alone on them, but on those who have tested them, who know their worth, and who can understandingly urge them forward. It is those who perform faithfully their appointed work from day to day, who in God's own time will hear His call, 'Come up higher.' "—*The Ministry of Healing*, p. 477.

All of us are vessels whom the Master desires to use, and He will use us in the way in which we are best fitted. "Every man has his place in the eternal plan of heaven. Whether we fill that place depends upon our own faithfulness in co-operating with God."—*Ibid.*, p. 476. Many a man has disqualified himself from greater responsibility by attempting to do his hoped-for next job, at the same time neglecting or performing inefficiently his present one.

Christian Virtues

Optimistic as he was about the future of the young Christian church, Paul was under no illusions about the efforts of Satan to lure away the Christians on whom the growth of the church depended. We noticed in the last chapter his sad allusion to a former worker who had left to work for the world.

In his last "prison epistle," he urges Timothy to "flee . . . youthful lusts" and develop virtues that will withstand the assaults of the devil.

Virtuous youth. 2 Timothy 2:22.

While the word *virtue* has the root meaning of manliness, this property is by no means absent from women. It implies strength in the sense that a man is physically stronger, generally speaking, than a woman, and therefore able to bear heavier burdens. Virtue, however, is moral strength, those good qualities that are to be seen in human beings of either sex.

Peter listed eight characteristics in what we call a ladder. See 2 Peter 1:5-8. Paul referred to several similar characteristics in his second epistle to Timothy.

Peter contrasted his list with "corruption that is in the world through lust." Verse 4. Paul likewise contrasted the virtues which he extolled with the opposite qualities that are natural to fallen mankind. He advised: "Flee also youthful lusts." 2 Timothy 2:22.

Dallying with the enticements of Satan is an invitation to disaster, as Joseph realized when Potiphar's wife placed him in a compromising situation. He chose to flee, not stopping to explain. He had the ideal of purity in his mind's eye, and this temptress was obscuring his vision.

It is important to notice that it is much easier to flee from wrong when one has a positive objective to follow. Fleeing *to* virtue and godliness enables us to travel in the right direction *from* lust and vice. Paul made this perfectly plain, for he followed his admonition to flee from youthful lusts with a direct command to follow various positive virtues which we will examine in further detail.

First notice the expression "youthful lusts." While age and seniority are not exempt from temptations of this nature, it is certain that youth are particularly susceptible, for they walk untried paths, and vice allures. Youth are the strength of the church of the future, which adds weight to the following appeal: "The burden-bearers among us are falling in death. Many of those who have been foremost in carrying out the reform instituted by us as a people, are now past the meridian of life, and are declining in physical and mental strength. With the deepest concern the question may be asked, Who will fill their places? To whom are to be committed the vital interests of the church when the present standard-bearers fall? We cannot but look anxiously upon the youth of to-day as those who must take these burdens, and upon whom responsibilities must fall. These must take up the burden where others leave it, and their course will determine whether morality, religion, and vital godliness shall prevail, or whether immorality and infidelity shall corrupt and blight all that is valuable. Those who are older must educate the youth, by precept and example."—*Gospel Workers*, p. 68.

"A good character must be built up brick by brick. . . . The characters of Joseph and Daniel are good models for them [the youth] to follow, and in the life of the Saviour they have a perfect pattern."—*Ibid*., p. 69. Jesus Himself likened His followers to branches of the vine. See John 15:1-11. If these remain attached, they will bear rich fruit, the virtues of a life lived wholly for and in Christ.

Righteousness.

In a sense, this virtue is a composite of all the others, for it implies complete development of every characteristic. There are, however, two kinds, Israel's righteousness and God's. See Romans 10:3. Jesus said that the righteousness of the scribes and Pharisees did not qualify them for entrance into the kingdom of heaven. See Matthew 5:20. Later, in His Sermon on the Mount, He instructed us to "seek . . . first the kingdom of God, and his righteousness." Matthew 6:33. Righteousness implies strict obedience to God's commands, irrespective of outward appearance. Eve considered the fruit of the forbidden tree in Eden to be attractive (it was!) even though it was fatal to eat it. Abel's offering of a lamb presents a gruesome picture compared with the unspoiled fruit that Cain placed upon his altar. But the latter was contrary to divine instruction and demonstrated human works of righteousness, whereas the symbolism of the slain lamb showed the substitutionary righteousness of the perfect Lamb of God. Hence, in spite of appearances, "Abel offered unto God a more excellent sacrifice" (Hebrews 11:4) and earned the commendation of "righteous" through Christ's merits.

Faith.

Abraham was distinguished by his faith, and those who follow him in exercising faith are called his children. "They which are of faith, the same are the children of Abraham." "So then they which be of faith are blessed with faithful Abraham." Galatians 3:7, 9. His faith faltered at times, it is true, as when he uttered the half-truth concerning Sarah, his half-sister and also his wife.

But we tend to accuse him of faithlessness when he waited long for the fulfillment of the promise of a son. However, careful reading of his experience reveals that his faith was increasing step by step, for he believed God even though his having a son seemed utterly impossible. When he was 75 years old, God promised to make of him a great nation. See Genesis 12:2, 4. This implied the birth of a son, but God did not specifically say so. Years went by. God repeated the promise after Abram—as he was known then—rescued Lot, but there was no sign of any son arriving. Abram suggested that in harmony with the custom of the times he might adopt Eliezer, his steward. See Genesis 15:2, 3. This was not acceptable to God, and the Lord made a more specific promise: "Out of thine own bowels shall be thine heir." Verse 4. This meant that an adoption was ruled out and that Abram himself was to be the father; but God made no mention of the mother.

Again there was a waiting period until Sarai, who no longer believed that she could bear a son, offered a solution. Abram agreed. He took Sarai's servant, Hagar, and "out of his own bowels" produced an heir. Genesis 16:2-4. So when he was 86 years old Abram had a son, Ishmael. He soon realized that this was not the child of promise, and for 13 more years his faith was tested until the Lord gave even more detailed information. This time He mentioned Sarai's name and changed it to Sarah: "Sarah thy wife shall bear thee a son indeed." Genesis 17:19. So now both father and mother and the son who was to be born were named. See Genesis 17:19.

Abraham was Abram's new name, and he demonstrated his growing faith by submitting to circumcision, along with Ishmael and the other males of his large household. Step by step his faith had increased as he accepted ever more difficult conditions. Some twenty years after Isaac's birth (see *Patriarchs and Prophets*, p. 147) he passed the supreme test, "the closest which man was ever called to endure."—*Ibid*. His faith by now was so strong that Abraham "staggered not." He believed he would receive Isaac back from the dead. See Hebrews 11:19.

Love.

There is little doubt that if a survey were taken to find which virtue was the most desirable, the votes would score heavily in favor of love. It is the gift Paul told us to covet earnestly. It excels even faith and hope and is equated with the Godhead, for "love is of God" and "God is love." 1 John 4:7, 8.

God even loved sinners who rebelled against Him, which is a true test of real love. Love works miracles; it calls forth love where only enmity existed before. "We love him, because he first loved us." 1 John 4:19. The supreme act of love is commemorated each Easter in special services. It is the theme of Isacc Watts' grand hymn:

> When I survey the wondrous cross
> On which the Prince of glory died,
> My richest gain I count but loss,
> And pour contempt on all my pride.

Were the whole realm of nature mine,
That were a tribute far too small;
Love so amazing, so divine,
Demands my life, my soul, my all.
—*The Church Hymnal*, no. 120

Love is the antithesis of selfishness, the characteristic so prominent in Lucifer. When Isaiah saw the origin of the great controversy in heaven, he put into the mouth of the covering cherub a series of *I's*. Not for Lucifer, the second place! Never would he submit to Christ! Leadership of the heavenly host was not sufficient for his pride. "I will ascend . . . ; I will exalt . . . ; I will sit . . . ; I will ascend . . . ; I will be." Isaiah 14:13, 14.

Jonathan exhibited a marvelously self-denying love toward David, though he knew David would succeed his father in the kingship instead of himself. Jonathan showed no jealousy at all. Time and again, when by simply doing nothing he could have left David's life in grave danger, he intervened to spare his friend from the insane wrath of Saul. Here then lay a serious dilemma for the young prince, a clash between loyalty to his father the king on one hand, and loyalty to his friend David on the other.

Notice the many occasions when love triumphed over selfishness in his life. He gave his royal robe and special weapons to David. See 1 Samuel 18:4. He refused to carry out his father's command to kill David. Chapter 19:1. Instead, he alerted David to the threat so that he could hide, then pleaded with his father to change his mind. Verses 4-6. Later Jonathan made excuses for David's absence from the feast of the new moon, which so enraged Saul that he hurled his javelin at his son. See 1 Samuel 20:28-33.

Still Jonathan maintained his covenant with his friend, and at a time when Saul and his soldiers were hunting David "every day" (1 Samuel 23:14), he risked a secret meeting with David "and strengthened his hand in God." Verse 16. He said to David, "Thou shalt be king over Israel, and I shall be next unto thee; and that also Saul my father knoweth." Verse 17.

Jonathan showed magnificently the qualities of the friend of the bridegroom described later by John the Baptist: "The friend of the bridegroom, which standeth and heareth him, rejoiceth greatly because of the bridegroom's voice: this my joy therefore is fulfilled. He must increase, but I must decrease." John 3:29, 30.

Jonathan evidently resolved his conflict between love for David and loyalty to the throne, for he joined his father in the last fateful battle on Mount Gilboa. See 1 Samuel 31:1, 2. It was Jonathan who evoked the famous words of the lament, used even today: "How are the mighty fallen." 2 Samuel 1:27. Is it any wonder that "the name of Jonathan is treasured in heaven, and it stands on earth a witness to the existence and the power of unselfish love."—*Education*, p. 157.

Peace.

Our planet is at war with God. Since the first transgression, man has never lived at peace with his neighbor. It is a human characteristic to stand up for one's rights. In a society of selfish individuals, this is bound to lead to conflict, and the history of nations is a sad story of man striving for power and for the possessions of others.

A conflict between two persons is regrettable enough. But how disastrous it becomes when it involves communities and nations and forces individuals to kill those against whom they have no personal animosity. War is the devil's toy. He uses it to inflame the hostile thoughts and vicious deeds to which mankind is prone.

"Satan delights in war, for it excites the worst passions of the soul and then sweeps into eternity its victims steeped in vice and blood. It is his object to incite the nations to war against one another, for he can thus divert the minds of the people from the work of preparation to stand in the day of God."—*The Great Controversy*, p. 589.

What a tremendous contrast was the message of the angels when our Saviour was born in Bethlehem! They sang: "on earth peace, good will toward men." Luke 2:14. He who had arrived was the "Prince of Peace," and "of the increase of his government and peace there shall be no end." Isaiah 9:6, 7.

The followers of this Man of peace will exalt this Christian virtue and practice the counsel of Paul to the Romans: "If it be possible, as much as lieth in you, live peaceably with all men." Romans 12:18. The other person may be antagonistic, but the Christian's attitude must not be retaliation but peace. Failure to seek peace will result in loss, for "a brother offended is harder to be won than a strong city." Proverbs 18:19. Manifesting a peaceful spirit under provocation may result in the conversion of a soul. This reign of peace is expressed by an unknown hymn writer:

> Gentle Peace, from heaven descended,
> We would live beneath Thy law;
> Thou hast home and life befriended,
> Born of nobler deeds than war.

> Stay Thou with us, still replenish
> Fields with fruit, ourselves with love;
> Discord and dissension banish,
> Peaceful Spirit from above.
> —*The Church Hymnal*, no. 511

This is the wisdom from above which is pure, peaceable, and gentle; impartial, merciful, and fruitful. See James 3:17.

Gentleness.

The root meaning of the word *gentle* as Paul used it in Second Timothy is "not saying a word." Do not answer roughly when spoken to roughly; give the "soft answer" that "turneth away wrath," for "grievous words stir up anger." Proverbs 15:1. This idea persists in diplomatic circles, where it is customary to use kind, tactful words when expressing distasteful messages. The characteristic, when exemplified in human beings—alas, all too rarely—has given us the words *gentleman* and *gentlewoman*, connoting a man or a woman who always speaks the truth, keeps his or her word, and is kind and gracious to everyone. Further facets of a gentleman or a gentlewoman are listed in Psalm 15, which has been called the gentleman's psalm.

Gentlemen are assumed to be men in high society and paragons of virtue, but unfortunately this is not always the case. The high ideals of the legendary knights of old—courtesy, gallantry, trustworthiness, honesty, sincerity, faithfulness, and the like—are rarely seen today. The stark contrast between ideals and behavior prompted Edmund Burke's ironic comment, "Somebody has said, that a king may make a nobleman, but he cannot make a gentleman."—*Letter*, 29 January 1795. God alone gives the gentle spirit, for it is an ingredient of the divine "wisdom that is from above," "gentle, and easy to be intreated." James 3:17. The renowned headmaster of Rugby School, Thomas Arnold (1795-1852), wrote in the school's objectives: "What we must look for here is, first, religious and moral principles; secondly, gentlemanly conduct; thirdly, intellectual ability." In the light of eternal values, his priorities cannot be faulted. They lead to happy, contented living here and hereafter.

Patience and longsuffering.

It is not easy to distinguish between patience and longsuffering. The Greek *hupomone* is translated in the New Testament 28 times as patience. Another word, *makrothumia*, is translated 13 times as longsuffering and five times as patience. The second word gives the idea of waiting a long time before becoming passionate or breathing hard, whereas the first has the root meaning of undergoing, or remaining under. Paul uses both words in 2 Timothy 3:10, so he must have recognized a distinction between them. His life as a Christian was in marked contrast to his attitude as a Jew.

"Patience and gentleness under wrong were not characteristics prized by the heathen or by the Jews. The statement made by Moses under the inspiration of the Holy Spirit, that he was the meekest man upon the earth, would not have been regarded by the people of his time as a commendation; it would rather have excited pity or contempt. But Jesus places meekness among the first qualifications for His kingdom."—*Thoughts From the Mount of Blessing*, p. 14. Moses, "learned in all the wisdom of the Egyptians" (Acts 7:22), privileged to "speak mouth to mouth" (Numbers 12:8) with Jehovah, did not parade his learning but led his people patiently and with longsuffering. Job endured sufferings which he could not comprehend, waiting God's own time to understand. He said, "Though he slay me, yet will I trust in him." Job 13:15. He believed that "he knoweth the way that I take" (Job 23:10), even though Job himself could not discern God at his right or left, in front or behind (See verses 8, 9).

Noah is another excellent example of longsuffering. He was "a preacher of righteousness" (2 Peter 2:5) who had very little to show for more than a century of evangelism, while "the longsuffering [*makrothumia*] of God waited" (1 Peter 3:20). Noah tolerated both sinners and scoffers, but he faithfully rebuked their sin.

Most important, this quality of patience will mark the remnant who are faithful to their Lord. Under great stress, because they uphold the commandments given from Sinai, patiently enduring as they maintain the faith of Jesus, they call forth the tribute: "Here is the patience of the saints." Revelation 14:12.

Harmonious development.

All these virtues are, in a sense, fruits of the Spirit of God. They are not produced instantaneously as ripe fruit, for we are to "grow in grace, and in the knowledge of our Lord and Saviour Jesus Christ." 2 Peter 3:18. The natural man bears unripe fruit, but the miraculous working of the Spirit causes the fruit to ripen.

We are not to excel in one gift or fruit at the expense of the malfunction of another. Peter's ladder of virtues lists eight graces or virtues, and "giving all diligence" (2 Peter 1:5), we are to add one to another. The intent is not to perfect one and then proceed to perfect the second, and so on; for the little word in English, *add*, is the translation of a much longer Greek word which is composed of three other words. Its literal meaning is "to lead on in a dance or choir." The basic idea is that these eight virtues are not to be presented one by one, but rather as a composite whole. Just as a choir or an octet is not merely eight separate voices, but a harmonious blend of eight voices, the whole being greater than the sum of its parts, so the Christian virtues are to be blended in a harmonious combination leading ultimately to the "perfect man, unto the measure of the stature of the fullness of Christ." Ephesians 4:13. Paul's goal was to "present every man perfect in Christ Jesus . . . according to his working." Colossians 1:28, 29.

It is incongruous to visualize a Christian strong in faith but short-tempered, or one who is abundant in love but full of pride. As Peter rightly says: "If these things [virtues] be in you, and abound, they make you that ye shall neither be barren nor unfruitful in the knowledge of our Lord Jesus Christ." 2 Peter 1:8.

Avoiding Apostasy

Not everything in Paul's last letter is happy. One sad verse records the defection of a faithful helper. We can almost see tears glisten in the flickering candlelight as Paul dictates, "Demas hath forsaken me, having loved this present world."

Apostasy is a danger Paul knows will dog the church till the end of time. Timothy must not be disheartened if it takes some of his members. Paul prepares the young pastor by listing pressures and temptations that might cause the defection of even his most promising converts.

Last-day perils. 2 Timothy 3:1.

With the increase of knowledge, the mind of man, already set toward evil, has discovered more and more ways to counter God's plan. Once the devil has turned him away from God, man becomes bent on self-destruction, though he may not realize it.

It is to be expected, then, that in the days preceding the coming of our Lord "evil men and seducers shall wax worse and worse." 2 Timothy 3:13. "They have sown the wind, and they shall reap the whirlwind." Hosea 8:7.

Well may the unbeliever tremble as world conditions worsen, but these troubles should strengthen the Christian's faith, for they fulfill the words of our Lord when He said that "iniquity shall abound." Matthew 24:12. He also said that "the love of many shall wax cold." Verse 12. But He continued with the cheering statement that some would "endure unto the end." Verse 13.

External circumstances should not tempt us into carelessness and apostasy. They should stimulate us to avoid the seductions of the evil one and his emissaries and to remain true and faithful though others fall away. Clear warning is given as to the marks of apostasy, so that we need not be deceived when they are made to appear attractive.

Selfishness. 2 Timothy 3:2.

Selfishness is the root cause of sin. It was the ruin of Lucifer, the covering cherub. His way was best, he thought, and he owed no allegiance to anyone, not even to the God who had created him. He exercised his will on his own behalf, endeavoring to find a more exalted station than he possessed, even though he was already the leader of the heavenly host.

"In his heart there was a strange, fierce conflict. Truth, justice, and loyalty were struggling against envy and jealousy. . . . But again he was filled with pride in his own glory. His desire for supremacy returned, and envy of Christ was once more indulged."—*Patriarchs and Prophets*, p. 37. While this does not give a reason for the existence of sin, nor indeed can one be given, it does reveal that pride was the basis of this first transgression.

In loving mercy, Jehovah gave Satan opportunity to see the course he was pursuing, and Satan "nearly reached the decision to return; but pride forbade him."—*Ibid.*, p. 39. Pride is a manifestation of selfishness, the placing of ourself first. It is the very antithesis of the meek and lowly Jesus who "made himself of no reputation, and took upon him the form of a servant." Philippians 2:7.

There is an interesting difference in the grammar of the verb in English and other western languages, compared with Hebrew. In the former we conjugate the verb as: I am, you are, he is. We call the pronouns *I, you,* and *he* the first, second, and third persons. Hebrew is different. The verb is conjugated: He is, you are, I am. While Hebrew is not a sacred language, the fact that it is the language of most of the Old Testament could remind us of a spiritual truth that would curb our natural selfishness: *He* comes first and *I* come last, *you*, my neighbor, come in between.

Boasting is an outcome of selfishness. Babel was one of the first cities built for the grandeur of its builders. The founders said, "Let us make us a name." Genesis 11:4. So in later years its greatest king demonstrated self-pride when he exclaimed, "Is not this great Babylon, that I have built for the house of the kingdom by the might of my power, and for the honour of my majesty?" Daniel 4:30.

But Nebuchadnezzar showed that there was a cure for pride and boasting. After his miserable seven years learning the lessons of humility, he manifested true conversion as seen in his words: "Now I Nebuchadnezzar praise and extol and honour the King of heaven, all whose works are truth, and his ways judgment: and those that walk in pride he is able to abase." Daniel 4:37. He directed praise and honor and glory outward *from* himself to the One to whom all praise belongs.

"The once proud monarch had become a humble child of God; the tyrannical, overbearing ruler, a wise and compassionate king. He who had defied and blasphemed the God of heaven, now acknowledged the power of the Most High. . . . This public proclamation, in which Nebuchadnezzar acknowledged the mercy and goodness and authority of God, was the last act of his life recorded in sacred history."—*Prophets and Kings*, p. 521.

Boasting is truly a form of blasphemy, for it ignores God and places self first instead of the Creator. Pharaoh, another tyrannical monarch, boastfully insulted God. He sneered, "Who is Jehovah that I should obey his voice?" Exodus 5:2. Referring to the infidel leaders of the French Revolution and their deliberate flouting of God's authority, Ellen White wrote, "What an echo is this of the Pharaoh's demand: 'Who is Jehovah, that I should obey His voice?' . . . The Lord declares concerning the perverters of the truth: 'Their folly shall be manifest to all.' "—*The Great Controversy*, p. 275.

What blasphemous boasting appears in the story of the profane sea captain whose ship was delayed in port by fierce storms! "We shall sail," he said, "at daybreak tomorrow, God willing." Then with a show of defiance, he added, "and, in any case, at noon."

Truce-breaking is another by-product of selfishness. If one breaks his word, how can he be trusted later? If by virtue of self-interest, a man decides not to honor his promise, selfishness becomes his god, and he fails to qualify among those who "swear to their own hurt, and change not." Psalm 15:4. If one breaks his promise to a friend whom he can see, how much easier it is to break his promise to God whom he cannot see!

False accusations also grow from selfishness. It is a sign of coming apostasy when a church member begins accusing the brethren. No one is perfect, and those who hold responsible positions in the work of God would be the last to claim perfection. So mistakes will be made. But woe to the one who fastens on them and sees nothing else, who makes no allowance for the frailty of human nature, and who finally misjudges even those who are doing their best. Such are doing the devil's work, as depicted in Zechariah 3:1.

In this encouraging vision, Zechariah saw Joshua the high priest clothed in filthy garments, representing his own righteousness, and Satan, the adversary, standing nearby, accusing him and the nation whom he represented. The Lord rebuked Satan and robed the repentant sinner in garments of His own righteousness.

Incontinence is yet another outgrowth of selfishness. Samson, strong in physical power, became "weak, and . . . as another man" (Judges 16:7, 11) when Delilah had his locks shaved off. Actually, he was terribly weak before this episode, for he had no control over his passions. When these are unchecked, a man follows his own selfish desires regardless of the will of God.

Worldliness. 2 Timothy 3:4.

The world is set in opposition to the church. The church exists in this world, but it really belongs to the other, the perfect one promised by God for those who love Him. But one can be in the church and have one's name registered on its books and still be a worldling. Churchgoing is a good and desirable habit, but it is not synonymous with godliness. True, we measure godliness by externals, for who can judge motives? But external behavior must be prompted by internal conviction if it is to ensure true godliness. Otherwise it will be but a cloak, equivalent to the hypocrisy of the scribes who "make clean the outside of the cup and of the platter, but within they are full of extortion and excess." Matthew 23:25.

John showed the contrast when he wrote: "Love not the world, neither the things that are in the world." "The world passeth away." 1 John 2:15, 17. The things of time and sense are transient, even though they seem to have persisted for centuries. There is an eternity and a heaven to gain, and he who trades the seen for the unseen sells his soul in a cheap market.

The rich fool (see Luke 12:16-20) concerned himself only with the things of this life and with laying up treasure on earth, "where moth and rust doth corrupt, and where thieves break through and steal." Matthew 6:19. God's judgment of him was to call him a fool, unwise, shortsighted, living only in the present and for himself, saying "in his heart, There is no God." Psalm 14:1.

This "poor" man had a bumper harvest that filled his barns. Others accumulate even greater possessions and power, urged on by the prince of darkness. These may leave their names in secular history as great conquerors, having gained almost the whole world. But Jesus said, "What is a man profited, if he shall gain the whole world, and lose his own soul? or what shall a man give in exchange for his soul?" Matthew 16:26.

"At this time, before the great final crisis, as before the world's first destruction, men are absorbed in the pleasures and pursuits of sense. Engrossed with the seen and the transitory, they have lost sight of the unseen and eternal. For the things that perish with the using, they are sacrificing imperishable riches."—*Education*, p. 183. "We need to study the working out of God's purpose in the history of nations and in the revelation of things to come, that we may estimate at their true value things seen and unseen; that we may learn what is the true aim of life; that, viewing the things of time in the light of eternity, we may put them to their truest and noblest use."—*Ibid.*, p. 184.

Formalism. 2 Timothy 3:5.

Formalism is a deadly deception, a wolf in sheep's clothing. It has all the appearance of godliness, but it is a hollow sham. "To substitute external forms of religion for holiness of heart and life, is still as pleasing to the unrenewed nature as it was in the days of these Jewish teachers [in Galatia]. Today, as then, there are false spiritual guides, to whose doctrines many listen eagerly."—*The Acts of the Apostles*, p. 387.

Note that it is not the forms of religion that are at fault, it is their substitution for true heart religion. Forms of worship may assist a worshiper, but they are in themselves not Christian experience. The Jews were entrenched in formalism. They had multiplied rites and ceremonies and taught that these were the essentials of religion, whereas they were nothing more than man's inventions, collections of traditional rubbish. Jesus likened them to dried-up wineskins that could not contain new truth.

Hardened and blinded by their false interpretation of the coming Messiah, the Jewish leaders were not given the glorious news of His birth. Instead, this divine revelation was given to humble shepherds of the chosen race, and to wise men born outside the commonwealth of Israel.

Formalism is a matter of externals, of the body, whereas true religion is a matter of the internal, of the heart, of submission to the will of God. "Lovers of pleasure may put on a form of godliness that involves some self-denial even, and they may sacrifice time and money, and yet self not be subdued, and the will not be brought into subjection to the will of God."—*Testimonies for the Church*, vol. 3, p. 29.

We can see a powerful illustration in the experiences of John and Judas. Both lived in close companionship with Jesus. Both were His disciples. Yet their lives demonstrate the vivid contrast between sanctification and formalism. "In striking contrast to the sanctification worked out in the life of John is the experience of his fellow-disciple Judas. Like his associate, Judas professed to be a disciple of Christ, but he possessed only a form of godliness. . . . Instead of walking in the light, he chose to walk in darkness. . . . John and Judas are representatives of those who profess to be Christ's followers. . . . Each possessed serious defects of character; and each had access to the divine grace that transforms character. But while one in humility was learning of Jesus, the other revealed that he was not a doer of the word, but a hearer only."—*The Acts of the Apostles*, pp. 557, 558.

Another danger of religious formalism is that it tends to retain in the church those who are self-satisfied and smug and who appear to be models of righteousness. At the same time it keeps out of the church those who see the shams and the shame of nominal Christians who are not living up to their profession. The vile profligate is easily seen for what he is, for he makes no profession; but the thin veneer and disguise covering a formal Christian is a dishonor to the church he represents.

Too often today, as when Moses was on Mount Sinai communing with the Eternal One, Christ's followers give themselves up to ecstatic forms of worship, bowing before golden calves. In Israel's later history, the ark became an object of worship. Many Israelites deemed it to have miraculous power to deliver them from their enemies. But it failed in Eli's time, for the people were disobedient to the sacred law contained within the ark. Without obedience to the law, the ark was of about as much value to them as would have been any other wooden box of the same size and shape. "Their very worship of the ark led to formalism, hypocrisy, and idolatry. . . . It was not enough that the ark and the sanctuary were in the midst of Israel. It was not enough that the priests offered sacrifices, and that the people were called the children of God."—*Patriarchs and Prophets*, p. 584. What was required was a departure from the formalism of the day and a return to a circumcision of the heart and ears (see Acts 7:51) and a loving obedience to the will of God.

The vast material growth of the Adventist Church, seen in its massive institutions, its health-food industry, its publishing houses, its schools and universities, its churches and hospitals, is a sign of the blessing of God. But it can also encourage a religious formalism. These accessories to the preaching of the gospel were designed to help call out a people who would make Christ first and best in everything. Anyone who, impressed by these externals, joins the church without a renewal of heart and mind becomes a source of weakness to the church. It is possible to go through the forms and ceremonies and practices of the church without ever really doing them with a heart full of love for Christ and an understanding of their spiritual significance. How careful we must all be to avoid this very subtle form of deception in these last days!

False teachings.

With a solid foundation of truth on which to build, and with doctrines that have been forged by deep study of God's Word, it seems impossible that believers should be tossed to and fro, carried about with every wind of doctrine. See Ephesians 4:14. Yet it has been foretold, and it has surely come to pass. Satan has been almost as successful here as he was in Eden, where he used apparent evidence to contradict the clear statements of God. Today the introduction of a little error or doubt into a whole mass of truth easily deceives the unwary. Attracted by the plausibility of a new "truth," swept along by the enthusiasm of the one who peddles it, the believer acts like the captain of a ship who relies on a faulty compass. Following what he sincerely believes to be a safe guide, he sees his vessel dashed on the rocks, making shipwreck of his life.

If new teachings were full of error, they would be easily discerned and rejected. It is the subtle mixture of much truth with a little speculation that sows poisonous seeds in the human heart. This attraction for false teaching comes about partly as a feeling of superiority in possessing extra knowledge, partly because of the possession of what Paul called "itching ears." 2 Timothy 4:3. Such ears delight to accept fables rather than truth and the pure word of God. It is a clever deception of the enemy not to cause people to disbelieve, but rather to persuade them to "believe a lie." 2 Thessalonians 2:11. It is the end result of not receiving "the love of the truth, that they might be saved." Verse 10.

The literal translation of "itching ears" is "tickling the hearing," and Moffatt renders it "tickle their own fancies." Fables tickle the ears, but truth transforms the heart.

There is a great temptation to hear only what we want to hear. This is often seen in those seeking counsel. How often we go for advice to counselors who we think will speak in harmony with our unexpressed desires. Then our preconceived ideas receive the weight of independent authority, and we are confirmed in what could well be unbelief. The only true, infallible touchstone is the Word of God interpreted by itself and sealed by the gift of the Spirit to him who follows the divine leading.

The perils of the last days are the final acts in the great controversy between God and Satan. Each is seeking to gain man for his kingdom, and the controlling forces employed are love on the one hand and compulsion on the other. Truth is on one side and error and deception on the other. To fall away from truth is to accept apostasy. The outcome of these issues determines our eternal destiny.

God and Satan are both engaged in taking men alive, Satan by appealing to man's lower nature, and God by appealing through His great love to man's spiritual sensibilities. The word translated "taken captive" (2 Timothy 2:26) literally means "taken alive." It is used only one other time in the New Testament and, significantly, is applied to God's call to mankind. When calling the disciples, Jesus said to Simon Peter: "Fear not; from henceforth thou shalt catch men." Luke 5:10. So Peter, and with him all other gospel workers, were to catch men alive and take them out of the snare of Satan who is engaged in precisely the same occupation. Apostasy consists of being taken prisoner by Satan, and the gospel messenger preaches "deliverance to the captives." Luke 4:18.

The battle for the soul. 2 Timothy 2:26.

A tense battle rages for the possession of human hearts. The deciding factor is the individual's choice. The battle ceases only when the man dies. John Bunyan gives a splendid allegory in his book, *The Holy War*. The city of Mansoul, with its Eargate and Eyegate, Mouthgate, Nosegate, and Feelgate, seized by Diabolus, is finally recaptured by Prince Emmanuel and his generals Boanerges, Conviction, and others.

"Enslaved by sin, the moral powers are under the tyranny of Satan. The soul is made the sport of his temptations; and unless some mighty arm is stretched out to rescue him, man goes where the arch-rebel leads the way."—*Testimonies for the Church*, vol. 7, p. 42. May God take us alive out of the net of sin!

Keeping the Faith

The last chapter of the Second Epistle to Timothy contains the last written words of Paul that we possess. They therefore carry greater importance, because he knew that his end was near and that he would not have the opportunity very much longer to write, preach, and counsel.

A living witness.
This epistle is, so to speak, Paul's last will and testament. It is a fitting epitaph. So are his words, written in Greek and English, on a large stone in the ruins of old Corinth: "For this slight momentary affliction is preparing for us an eternal weight of glory beyond all comparison." 2 Corinthians 4:17.

That statement sums up Paul's attitude to life. Nothing could swerve him from the Damascus vision. All that the devil could do to dissuade him, by persecution, by slander, by imprisonment, by false brethren, was as nothing to the immeasurable joy he anticipated when at last he would be home with his Saviour.

His one main concern now was that others would take up the challenge and continue to expand the work he had so faithfully begun, and carry the gospel to the ends of the earth. He hoped that his death as well as his life would be a perpetual stimulus to others to follow his example.

Not all epitaphs are as true as Paul's. While it is an excellent motto to speak "nothing but good of the dead," this maxim has been carried to such extremes that epitaphs are often filled with fulsome flattery; the qualities attributed to the departed bear but little relation to their life-style. What a shining example, however, we have in Paul.

And we have a similar example in a patriarch who lived at a time of increasing corruption and ungodliness. It is written of Enoch that "before his translation he had this testimony, that he pleased God." Hebrews 11:5. While living on earth in the midst of iniquity he merited this wonderful description.

"The wickedness of men had reached such a height that destruction was pronounced against them. As year after year passed on, deeper and deeper grew the tide of human guilt, darker and darker gathered the clouds of divine judgment. Yet Enoch, the witness of faith, held on his way, warning, pleading, entreating, striving to turn back the tide of guilt, and to stay the bolts of vengeance. Though his warnings were disregarded by a sinful, pleasure-loving people, he had the testimony that God approved, and he continued to battle faithfully against the prevailing evil, until God removed him from a world of sin to the pure joys of heaven."—*Patriarchs and Prophets*, p. 87. What an example for us who live when sin and rebellion are filling their cup against the Most High and we are to keep ourselves unspotted from the evil around us.

We must witness positively for truth, as well as avoid evil. It is our responsibility to warn the careless, the selfish, and the sinful that Jesus is coming soon. This is a work that angels would delight to do, but it is commissioned to human beings.

Preach the word. 2 Timothy 4:2.

An allegorical story tells of Jesus after His ascension. He is walking the streets of the Holy City in conversation with Gabriel. The latter has viewed all the events of Christ's life on earth and is now perplexed. He asks what provision the Master has made for His saving gospel to be carried to the millions of people who have never visited Palestine and are not of the Jewish race. Jesus replies that He told Peter and John and the other disciples to carry the news around the world. Gabriel asks: "But suppose they fail?" The answer, solemnizing to every Christian, comes: "I have no other plan."

Because preaching is a public ministry, some confuse it with public speaking. It is public speaking, but much more than that! Preaching is concerned with the exposition of the Word of God. It is treacherous to its name if it deals with secular subjects or current issues only. Its authority is the Word of God, and its expositor is a servant of the Most High. While social problems, economic issues, and political crises are proper topics of debate, they are secondary to the preaching of the Word of God. When Jesus was on earth He made no reference to slavery, He refused to enter into a legal argument concerning a brother's inheritance, He did not denounce the Roman occupation, He did not speak of the unfair distribution of wealth. But He did speak of serving God, He did advise peaceful submission to the powers that be, He did point out the folly of trusting in riches.

The kingdom of heaven.

Jesus preached time and again about His kingdom, His spiritual kingdom, that is. He never discussed the territorial boundaries of the realm of Israel at the time. Matthew collected some of the Lord's sayings in his thirteenth chapter. The key word is *kingdom*. When His disciples asked why He taught in parables, He said He wished to explain to them "the mysteries of the kingdom of heaven." Matthew 13:11. In explaining the parable of the sower He said: "When any one heareth the word of the kingdom." Verse 19. He introduced the parable of the tares: "The kingdom of heaven is likened. . . . " Verse 24. The parables of the mustard seed, the leaven, the hid treasure, the merchant man, the net (verses 31, 33, 44, 45, 47)—all five begin with the same formula: "The kingdom of heaven is like unto. . . . " In the same chapter are the expressions: "children of the kingdom" (verse 38), "gather out of his kingdom" (verse 41), "shine forth as the sun in the kingdom" (verse 43), and "every scribe which is instructed unto the kingdom of heaven" (verse 52). The constant repetition is not really surprising, for "Jesus came into Galilee, preaching the gospel of the kingdom." Mark 1:14. He taught us to pray, "Thy kingdom come." Matthew 6:10.

Evidently, if we are following the Master's example, we shall be preaching about the kingdom—the kingdom of grace already established, and the kingdom of glory so soon to be set up. And our knowledge of the kingdom will be obtained from the Word of God, from the Old and New Testaments, both of which are studded with references to it. As His servants, He may use us to fulfill His prophecy, "This gospel of the kingdom shall be preached. . . ; and then shall the end come." Matthew 24:14.

Critics say that religion is the opiate of the people, that it is a device to divert the attention of the poor and oppressed from their miserable lot, to assure them of pie in the sky by and by. But the Word of God offers a better solution to earth's problems; it gives the believer satisfaction in this life as well as promise for the world to come. It has been said that the preaching of the Wesley brothers in the eighteenth century—and it was sound, biblical preaching—saved England from a blood bath similar to that which France suffered during the French Revolution. These gallant preachers lifted the minds of the poor from their misery, for they had been denied the gospel message because of their low station in life. The Wesleys gave them new hope, proving to them that God loved them and had called them to sonship with Him.

Personal Bible study.

Although the injunction "preach the word" applies in the first instance to those who minister in the pulpit, it has a secondary application to those who sit in the pew. The latter must feed on the bread of life and not on the husks of man's philosophy. It behooves them therefore, even though they hear the Word of God preached from the pulpit, to make it the man of their counsel in their daily lives. They must read and study the Bible by themselves and find in it the Word incarnate. It is so easy to take one's ease and depend on the pastor to offer the bread of life, whereas it is essential that each believer find the manna for himself as well.

"A day is coming . . . when all will wish to be thoroughly furnished by the plain, simple truths of the word of God, that they may meekly, yet decidedly, give a reason of their hope. This reason of their hope . . . they must have to strengthen their own souls for the fierce conflict."—*Testimonies for the Church*, vol. 1, p. 135.

Today the Bible is not restricted; it has been printed, either in part or in whole, in most of the world's languages and dialects in preparation for the time when "the everlasting gospel" shall be preached "unto them that dwell on the earth, and to every nation, and kindred, and tongue, and people." Revelation 14:6. How can we obey God and worship Him if we do not know His Word? How can we avoid the deceptions of the evil one if we do not know the Scriptures? "None but those who have fortified the mind with the truths of the Bible will stand through the last great conflict."—*The Great Controversy*, p. 593.

In season, out of season. 2 Timothy 4:2.

Be ready at every opportunity, whether it seems favorable or otherwise, to preach the Word, says Paul. He gave good examples of this in his own experience, as when he stood before Agrippa and Festus. He knew that what he said on this occasion would form the substance of the charge Festus would send to Caesar. It seems to us hardly the time to preach a sermon on the resurrection, but Paul did just that by weaving this truth into the story of his rejection and opposition by his own race. Festus, the Roman, considered this talk about Jesus of Nazareth's rising from the dead to be utter madness and interrupted loudly. But Paul seized the opportunity, evidently seeing some reaction on the face of Agrippa, to make a direct appeal to him: "King Agrippa, believest thou the prophets? I know that thou believest." Acts 26:27. Then he made an eloquent appeal to him, and to Bernice, the queen, to the chief captains, and to the principal men of the city (see Acts 25:23), that they might be Christians as he was, "except these bonds" (Acts 26:29).

"The whole company had listened spellbound to Paul's account of his wonderful experiences. The apostle was dwelling upon his favorite theme. None who heard him could doubt his sincerity." —*The Acts of the Apostles*, p. 437. Almost, almost Paul won a convert in these unusual surroundings. "But Agrippa put aside the proffered mercy, refusing to accept the cross" though he "might in justice have worn the fetters that bound the apostle."—*Ibid.*, p. 438.

Later, on the ship that was taking him to Rome, when it seemed a violent storm would overwhelm the vessel and everyone would be drowned, Paul expressed his faith in God. Amid the prevailing panic he announced, "Be of good cheer: for I believe God." Acts 27:25.

In Philippi, Paul and Silas seized the opportunity to convert the jailer. "They spake unto him the word of the Lord, and to all that were in his house." Acts 16:32. An earthquake had just shaken the city, but the most important work for Paul amid the rubble and confusion was to minister to a soul searching for salvation.

Reproof and rebuke.

How easy it is to offer rebuke or censure! The beam in our own eye is so large that it blocks our vision, but not sufficiently to obscure the mote that we preceive in our neighbor's eye! The counsel our Lord gave in the Sermon on the Mount (see Matthew 7:3-5) should be carefully regarded by those in authority, although this does not mean that reproof should never be given. Enoch, for example, was not a perfect man; but he was a holy one. "In the land where Cain had sought to flee from the divine presence, the prophet of God made known the wonderful scenes that had passed before his vision."—*Patriarchs and Prophets*, p. 86.

Enoch proclaimed the coming of the Lord. "He was a fearless reprover of sin. While he preached the love of God in Christ . . . he rebuked the prevailing iniquity, and warned . . . that judgment would surely be visited upon the transgressor. It was the Spirit of Christ that spoke through Enoch."—*Ibid*.

Notice the difference between the sin and the sinner. The sin must be exposed, but the sinner exhorted and pleaded with to forsake the sin. Care, tact, and wisdom must be exercised by the one who is reproving. His own life must be exemplary. "When a crisis comes in the life of any soul, and you attempt to give counsel or admonition, your words will have only the weight of influence for good that your own example and spirit have gained for you. . . . You can not exert an influence that will transform others until your own heart has been humbled and refined and made tender by the grace of Christ."—*Thoughts From the Mount of Blessing*, pp. 127, 128.

In pointing out error there are two dangers: one, that we may be too severe; the other, that in showing compassion we may be too tolerant of sin. "To hate and reprove sin, and at the same time to show pity and tenderness for the sinner, is a difficult attainment. . . . We must guard against undue severity toward the wrongdoer, but we must also be careful not to lose sight of the exceeding sinfulness of sin. There is need of showing Christlike patience and love for the erring one, but there is also danger of showing so great toleration for his error that he will look upon himself as undeserving of reproof."—*The Acts of the Apostles*, pp. 503, 504. Hence Paul advised Timothy, not to reprove and rebuke only, but to "exhort with all longsuffering." 2 Timothy 4:2. The apostle was able to steer between the two extremes, for he became "all things to all men," that he might "by all means save some." 1 Corinthians 9:22. He placed himself in the position of the erring one and made it the chief objective of his reproof to save the soul. Reproving sinners may be one of the afflictions Paul exhorted Timothy to endure as he did the work of an evangelist. See 2 Timothy 4:5.

Cross and crown.

Poverty and suffering had been Paul's lot, abuse had been heaped upon him, his words had been distorted; but he continued to proclaim the gospel without fear or favor. He accepted trials as a part of his life and braved them in the strength of the Lord. "No cross, no crown. How can one be strong in the Lord without trials? To have strength we must have exercise. To have strong faith, we must be placed in circumstances where our faith will be exercised. . . . It is through much tribulation that we are to enter the kingdom of God. Our Saviour was tried in every possible way, and yet he triumphed in God continually. It is our privilege to be strong in the strength of God under all circumstances, and to glory in the cross of Christ."—*Testimonies for the Church*, vol. 3, p. 67.

The good fight of faith.

The three completed deeds of 2 Timothy 4:7 are very closely connected. The good fight is "the good fight of faith" (1 Timothy 6:12), and Paul had kept the faith while running his race. He had fulfilled the desire mentioned in his farewell address to the elders at Ephesus; namely, "that I might finish my course with joy, and the ministry." Acts 20:24. The ministry was the sharing of his faith and the implantation of that faith in the hearts of his converts. He had kept the faith, he had finished his course with joy, he had fought the good fight of faith.

Whether the Lord would grant him an extension of his already profitable life or whether He would release him from his earthly suffering was a matter of no moment to Paul. His sole desire was that "Christ shall be magnified in my body, whether it be by life, or by death. For to me to live is Christ, and to die is gain." Philippians 1:20, 21.

"If his Lord saw best for him to bear testimony through living and ministering, he would rightly represent Him. But the death of a righteous man can also be a powerful affirmation of the efficacy of the gospel of grace. The contrast between his death and the death of one who dies without hope would be so marked that its influence would bring gain for the kingdom of Christ."—*S.D.A. Bible Commentary*, vol. 7, p. 147.

With Paul's stirring example before us, we can sing from the heart the marching song of the Sunday School children written over one hundred years ago:

> Onward, Christian soldiers!
> Marching as to war,
> With the cross of Jesus
> Going on before.
> Christ, the royal Master,
> Leads against the foe;
> Forward into battle,
> See, His banners go!
>
> Crowns and thrones have perished,
> Kingdoms ruled and waned,
> But the church of Jesus
> Constant has remained.
> Gates of hell can never
> 'Gainst that church prevail;
> We have Christ's own promise,
> That can never fail.
> —*The Church Hymnal*, no. 360

What can we do but follow the rugged apostle's example!

The Christian's Hope

Whatever other factors contribute to Paul's cheerfulness in prison, none are more important than his confidence in the return of Jesus and the certainty of the resurrection. He does not see death as the door to life, but he believes that after his death, Jesus will come and restore him to life. He looks forward to living eternally with Jesus and the angels and all the vast unnumbered family of the redeemed.

Paul nowhere pictures this glorious future as restricted to himself and—perhaps—a few lucky friends. He assures Timothy that it is for "all them also that love his appearing." 2 Timothy 4:9. Because it is such a wonderful thing to look forward to, he elsewhere calls it the "blessed hope." Others quite appropriately call it the "Christian's hope." Think about it and read about it and pray about it until it becomes your hope too. Then, like Paul, you'll never despair again. And if, for the glory of God, you are ever put in prison, others will say of you as we say of Paul, the prisoner wouldn't cry!

A living hope.

Hope is positive, historically joined in Paul's song of love (1 Corinthians 13) with two other positive characteristics—faith and love. It takes on new meaning when we contrast it with its opposite, hopelessness. Without hope there is despair, defeat, no firm hold to cling to, no future prospect to look forward to.

The Bible uses hopelessness to describe the sinner who is far from God: he has "no hope," for he is "without God in the world." Ephesians 2:12. The cause is plainly stated; he is without God. The cure is simple, to be with God; for with God there is bright promise, future glory, a life of hope. Without God, a person is the sport of Satan, a puppet performing without a will of his own, or rather, a will so weak that it is controlled by the mastermind of Satan. His is a hopeless case; but thanks to the love of God and the sacrifice of Christ, there can be hope for such a one.

Death is a great sorrow to the loved ones left to mourn. Without a sure knowledge of the future and of the fate of the departed, there is anguish and hopelessness. But Christians have a lively hope which mitigates for them the sorrow that so often overwhelms "others which have no hope." 1 Thessalonians 4:13. Hope then, in an age of uncertainty and instability, is as solid as the anchor that keeps a ship safe from the rocks. It is "an anchor to the soul, both sure and stedfast." Hebrews 6:19.

This hope in a future life is well portrayed by John Bunyan in his famous allegory in the person of Hopeful, who joined Christian in his journey toward the Celestial City, because he had witnessed the martyrdom of Faithful in Vanity Fair: "for there was one whose name was Hopeful (being made so by the beholding of Christian and Faithful in their words and behaviour, in their suffering at the Fair), who joined himself unto him, and, entering into a brotherly covenant, told him that he would be his companion."—*Pilgrim's Progress*, p. 116. It was this same Hopeful who encouraged Christian when they were both immured in Doubting Castle, the fortress of Giant Despair. Death seemed imminent. Twice Hopeful raised the spirits of his companion and helped to chase away his gloom and discouragement and thoughts of suicide.

This kind of hope is sure and certain, not mere wishful thinking, again illustrated by Bunyan when he describes the two travelers passing through the river of death. "Hopeful also would endeavour to comfort him, saying, Brother, I see the gate, and men standing by to receive us; but Christian would answer, It is you, it is you they wait for; you have been Hopeful ever since I knew you."—*Ibid.*, p. 188.

Bunyan shows us how we can become full of hope and cast away our doubts by relating how Christian found the key, which he had possessed all the time! It unlocked all the doors and gates of Doubting Castle. It was called Promise.

The Comforter. 2 Timothy 4:17.
John wrote about the Comforter who would be sent to the disciples after the ascension of Christ. See John 16:7-15. A transliteration of the Greek word used for Comforter is *paraclete*, or one called to the side of. This same Comforter must have made His presence felt at Paul's first trial before Nero, for Paul told Timothy that although "all men forsook me," "the Lord stood with me." 2 Timothy 4:16, 17. There is a wealth of meaning in these words, for they present such a magnificent contrast: One Lord present with him more than compensated for all men's being absent.

There is even greater significance in the preposition *with*, for it is the same preposition which forms the first part, *para*, of the word *paraclete*. *Para* has several meanings, but in this context it means, beside, or in the presence of, as in the English word *parallel* which essentially means placed by the side of another, or as in *paramedic* which means one who helps beside the medical doctor. The Lord was *with* Paul, as the Comforter or Paraclete was *with* the disciples, and "if God be for us, who can be against us?" Romans 8:31.

Paul's hope in the Comforter was not misplaced, for He helped him answer effectively. He was "delivered out of the mouth of the lion." 1 Timothy 4:17. Paul may have been quoting Psalm 22:21: "Save me from the lion's mouth," thinking of his escape from Satan's plans to exterminate Christians, for "the devil, as a roaring lion, walketh about, seeking whom he may devour," according to his fellow worker, Peter. 1 Peter 5:8.

The fact that Paul was executed does not mean that the Comforter was not with him even at that time. The release from the first trial gave him freedom, to some extent, on this earth. Death gave him a greater release. For when Paul's mortal body perished, the hope that sustained him did not. His next thought after the ax fell will be the vision of the Lord descending in glory to welcome him to Paradise and the fulfillment of all his hopes. Such a hope is indeed "a lively hope." 1 Peter 1:3.

The gods of the heathen are so often capricious that their devotees are never sure when their deities are in a good mood or a bad one. Consequently, a large part of their worship consists in placating their gods by offerings designed to bring them into a generous frame of mind.

The Judge. 2 Timothy 4:8.

Those who do not know the true, kind, and loving God invest their deities with the same characteristics as humans possess. They live therefore in uncertainty, not knowing whether to expect blessing or cursing. Note in Paul's description that the Lord is a righteous Judge. 2 Timothy 4:8. His decisions are fair and consistent with His perfect character. He is infinitely superior to heathen deities, because He can read motives and search the innermost motives of the heart. As Hannah, the mother of Samuel, said in her prayer of rejoicing: "The Lord is a God of knowledge, and by him actions are weighed." 1 Samuel 2:3. The balances He uses are not like those of apostate Ephraim, "balances of deceit." Hosea 12:7. "A just weight and balance are the Lord's: all the weights of the bag are his work." Proverbs 16:11. We may be sure of justice when the Lord deals with us.

When the fingers of a man's hand wrote the fateful words on the plaster of Belshazzar's palace during his drunken orgy (see Daniel 5:5), the word TEKEL sealed the king's fate: "Thou art weighed in the balances, and art found wanting." Verse 27. With perfect weights and on a perfect balance the sentence pronounced was just.

> That night they slew him on his father's throne,
> The deed unnoticed and the hand unknown:
> Crownless and sceptreless Belshazzar lay,
> A robe of purple round a form of clay.
> —Edwin Arnold, quoted in *Thoughts on Daniel and the Revelation*, by Uriah Smith, p. 114.

Even today judges are symbols of equity, dispassionate justice, and fair pronouncements made without fear or favor. The confidence that we have a righteous Judge, assures us that, clothed with the righteousness of Christ, we will hear Him say to us, "Come, ye blessed of my Father, inherit the kingdom prepared for you from the foundation of the world." Matthew 25:34. "The

Lord Jesus Christ, who shall judge the quick and the dead at his appearing and his kingdom" (2 Timothy 4:1) is "the righteous judge" (verse 8) who accepts repentant sinners by virtue of His own righteous life. Our hope is in this just Judge. He has promised forgiveness, and He will fulfill His promise. In spite of protestations from the devil, the Lord maintains His righteous cause. Moses was a murderer (see Exodus 2:12), and murderers have their place outside the Holy City (see Revelation 22:15). But when Satan demanded his body, the Lord rebuked him and took Moses to heaven. See Jude 9; Luke 9:30. We may be sure that this incident will be repeated time and again. Satan will claim us as belonging to him, for we are sinners too. But our hope is in our righteous Judge, Michael the archangel. Jude 9. He will defend His own, for He has said, "Neither shall any man pluck them out of my hand." John 10:28. We can therefore look forward with confidence to the judgment as did Charles Wesley when he wrote:

Thou Judge of quick and dead,
Before whose bar severe,
With holy joy or guilty dread,
We all shall soon appear—
Our erring souls prepare
For that tremendous day,
And fill us now with watchful care,
And stir us up to pray.

Oh, may we all be found
Obedient to Thy word,
Attentive to the trumpet's sound.
And looking for our Lord.
—The New Advent Hymnal, no. 170

Our hope in the Judge will fill us with holy joy and dissipate all dread.

The resurrection.

Death is an enemy that will be swallowed up in victory. In this shadowed valley where we dwell, God's saints are laid to rest. Some die of old age; others are martyred for Christ's sake. Many die prematurely, smitten by fatal disease. In each case, the confident words of the apostle give hope of victory over the grave. His words, "Thanks be to God, which giveth us the victory through our Lord Jesus Christ" (1 Corinthians 15:57), are often used as a comfort and a challenge to our daily life in Christ. But essentially they refer to Paul's use of victory in verse 55: "O grave, where is thy victory?" Death is a temporary victory gained by Satan, but it is not the final end; a battle is lost, but the war will be won by Another.

The body decomposes in the tomb, but like a seed cast into the ground, it will spring into life at the call of the last trump. Eternal life is given to the believer when he accepts Christ. See John 3:36. After he dies, his life will respond to the call of the Life-giver. Then will begin the life without end, without sin, without fear, without sorrow or tears, the blessed hope of the resurrection from the dead. This was the promise to the faithful Israelites of old, who "having obtained a good report through faith, received not the promise: God having provided some better thing for us." Hebrews 11:39, 40. The Promised Land was one indeed flowing with milk and honey, but it had cemeteries. The New Jerusalem will not. And the garden of the new Eden will be a far better place than anything the Israelites ever dreamed about.

The crown of life.

It is interesting to observe that the crown of 2 Timothy 4:8 is the Greek word *stephanos*, from which, obviously, we get the Christian name Stephen. What a significant reminder this must have been to Paul! At the time of Stephen's martyrdom, he had watched over the clothes of those who stoned him. See Acts 7:58. Saul never forgot the saintly attitude of this Christian martyr; first, when "all that sat in the council, looking steadfastly on him, saw his face as it had been the face of an angel" (Acts 6:15), and second, hearing Stephen say, "I see the heavens opened, and the Son of man standing on the right hand of God," and "Lord, lay not this sin to their charge." Acts 7:56, 60.

So when Paul faced his executioners, he recalled the courage of Stephen and cast back his vision into the heavenly sanctuary where his Advocate, the Conqueror of death, was pleading for him. "Paul was taken in a private manner to the place of execution. Few spectators were allowed to be present; for his persecutors, alarmed at the extent of his influence, feared that converts might be won to Christianity by the scenes of his death. But even the hardened soldiers who attended him listened to his words and with amazement saw him cheerful and even joyous in the prospect of death. . . . More than one accepted the Saviour whom Paul preached, and erelong fearlessly sealed their faith with their blood."—*The Acts of the Apostles*, pp. 509, 510.

Courage begets courage, and God's truth, apparently defeated, surges onward with greater power. The death of Stephen "resulted in the conviction of Saul, who could not efface from his memory the faith and constancy of the martyr, and the glory that had rested on his countenance."—*Ibid.*, p. 101. That vision of the hope of the resurrection now sustained Paul in his final moments.

"A mightier than Satan had chosen Saul to take the place of the martyred Stephen, to preach and suffer for His name, and to spread far and wide the tidings of salvation through His blood."— *Ibid.*, p. 102. So the Christian has this wonderful hope that "maketh not ashamed." Romans 5:5. It was specifically stated by Paul when writing to Titus that it is a "hope of eternal life, which God, that cannot lie, promised." Titus 1:2. The word of the Almighty One is pledged to raise the righteous dead and award them at the resurrection with life immortal.

The King.

There is hope of reigning with Him (see 2 Timothy 2:12), for the redeemed in Revelation sing: Thou "hast made us unto our God kings and priests." Revelation 5:10. After the second advent of Christ they "reigned with Christ." Revelation 20:4. Paul's statement to Timothy is preceded by the assuring words, "It is a faithful saying," an expression which occurs in almost identical words four other times in Paul's pastoral epistles. See 1 Timothy 1:15; 3:1; 4:9; Titus 3:8. All refer to the future when the King shall take His own and reign in glory. All affirm Paul's confident hope in the King.

When Handel's *Messiah* was first performed in the presence of England's King George III, the monarch was so impressed by the Hallelujah Chorus with its repeated praise to the "King of kings, and Lord of lords," that he rose to his feet and remained standing until the chorus had concluded, a practice which has been followed by audiences ever since. The king recognized a greater King, to whom he owed allegiance and homage.

Kingship suggests princes and princesses. Every Christian is a son or daughter of God and has been promised an inheritance. It follows that each is a prince or a princess, an heir or an heiress of the King of kings. Furthermore, having confessed and accepted His name we are no longer "strangers and foreigners, but fellow-citizens with the saints, and of the household of God." Ephesians 2:19.

We are, in a sense, foreigners in this earth, because our citizenship is in heaven. See Philippians 3:20. We are thus living in a foreign country, ruled by the prince of this world. Actually, we are in enemy territory, for the ruler is at war with our King.

Our hope in our King includes the hope of a crown of glory (see 1 Peter 5:4), a crown of righteousness (2 Timothy 4:8), a crown of life (James 1:12), an incorruptible crown (1 Corinthians 9:25), a diadem which we will gladly cast at the feet of our King when our hopes are fulfilled (Revelation 4:10).

The blessed hope. 2 Timothy 4:7, 8.

Paul's famous trilogy appears again in 2 Timothy 4:7, 8, where he speaks of having kept the *faith*, and of having a firm *hope* in the crown laid up for him and for those that *love* His appearing. As long as we have hope, the future holds no terrors. Disappointment, persecution, disease, scorn, and loss may be our lot, but hope outshines them all. Oliver Goldsmith, in *The Captivity*, put into the mouth of the Hebrew captives in Babylon these words:

> Hope, like the gleaming taper's light,
> Adorns and cheers our way;
> And still, as darker grows the night,
> Emits a brighter ray.
> —*The Captivity,* II, lines 135-138.

One of the leaders of the infant church which later took the name of Seventh-day Adventists was Joseph Bates. He spent his considerable wealth advancing the cause he loved. But he always signed his letters, "Yours in the blessed hope." Many believe it is his experience that Annie Smith described in the first stanza of her hymn, "I Saw One Weary" (no. 371 in *The Church Hymnal*). The second and third stanzas probably refer respectively to James White, another pioneer leader, and to Annie Smith herself, who may have used masculine pronouns for disguise. The last stanza refers to all Christians and ends with the courageous words,

> O! what can buoy the spirits up?
> 'Tis this alone—the blessed hope.

Hope stirred the hearts of all who have gone before, trusting in the promises of God, knowing that what He had promised He was willing and able to perform. The blessed hope within their hearts kept them true to God, and unwittingly they set a pattern for us to follow.

> The Son of God goes forth to war,
> A kingly crown to gain;
> His blood-red banner streams afar:
> Who follows in His train?
>
> The martyr, first whose eagle eye
> Could pierce beyond the grave,
> Who saw his Master in the sky,
> And called on Him to save.
>
> A glorious band, the chosen few
> On whom the Spirit came;
> Twelve valiant saints, their hope they knew,
> And mocked the cross and flame;
>
> They met the tyrant's brandished steel,
> The lion's gory mane;
> They bowed their necks the stroke to feel;
> Who follows in their train?
>
> O God, to us may grace be given
> To follow in their train.
> —Reginald Heber, *The Church Hymnal*, no. 361